BLUE BOTTLE MYSTERY

THE GRAPHIC NOVEL

AN ASPERGER ADVENTURE

WRITTEN BY KATHY HOOPMANN

ADAPTED BY MIKE MEDAGLIA

ILLUSTRATED BY RACHAEL SMITH

JKP
Jessica Kingsley *Publishers*
London and Philadelphia

FIRST PUBLISHED IN 2016
BY JESSICA KINGSLEY PUBLISHERS
73 COLLIER STREET
LONDON NI 9BE, UK
AND
400 MARKET STREET, SUITE 400
PHILADELPHIA, PA 19106, USA

WWW.JKP.COM

ORIGINAL STORYLINE COPYRIGHT © KATHY HOOPMANN 2016
TEXT ADAPTATION COPYRIGHT © JESSICA KINGSLEY PUBLISHERS 2016
ILLUSTRATIONS COPYRIGHT © JESSICA KINGSLEY PUBLISHERS 2016

LIBRARY OF CONGRESS CATALOGING IN PUBLICATION DATA
A CIP CATALOG RECORD FOR THIS BOOK IS AVAILABLE FROM THE LIBRARY OF CONGRESS

BRITISH LIBRARY CATALOGUING IN PUBLICATION DATA
A CIP CATALOGUE RECORD FOR THIS BOOK IS AVAILABLE FROM THE BRITISH LIBRARY

ISBN 978 1 84905 650 2
EISBN 978 1 78450 204 1

PRINTED AND BOUND IN CHINA

CONTENTS

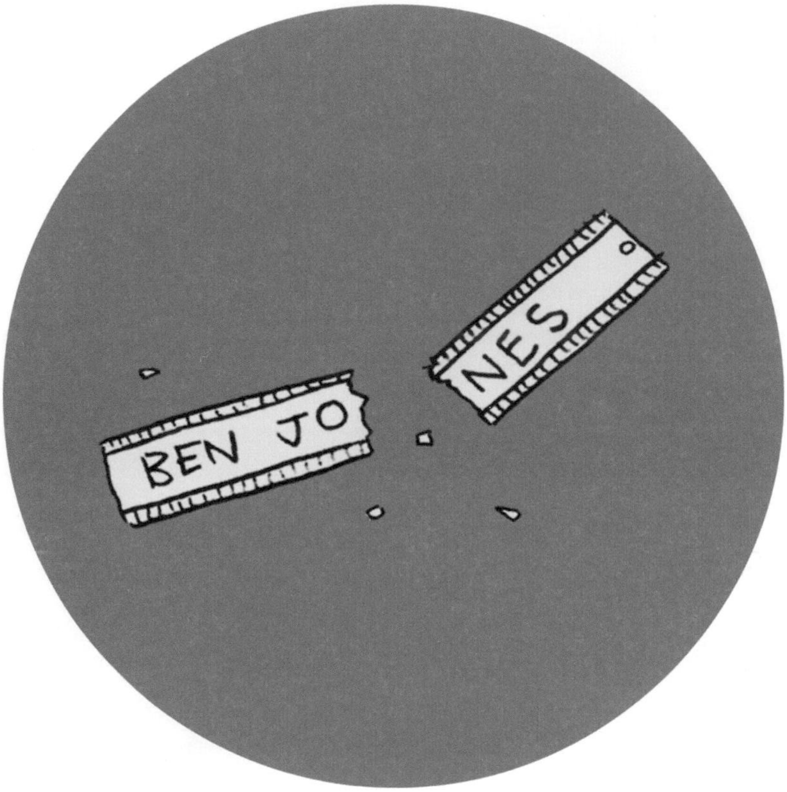
BEN JO
NES

CHAPTER 1: MISS BROWNING-LEVER

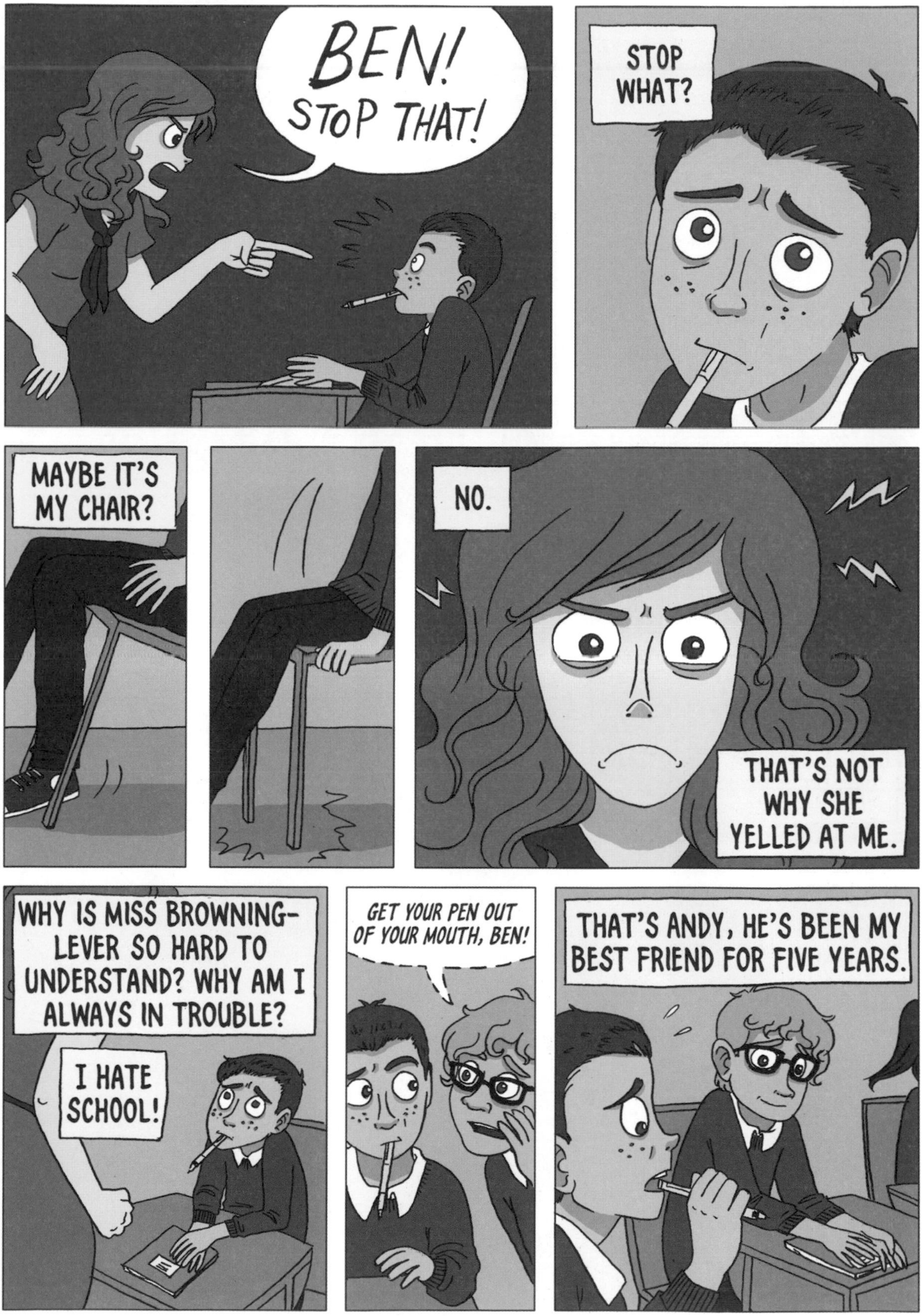
BEN! STOP THAT!
STOP WHAT?
MAYBE IT'S MY CHAIR?
NO.
THAT'S NOT WHY SHE YELLED AT ME.
WHY IS MISS BROWNING-LEVER SO HARD TO UNDERSTAND? WHY AM I ALWAYS IN TROUBLE?
I HATE SCHOOL!
GET YOUR PEN OUT OF YOUR MOUTH, BEN!
THAT'S ANDY, HE'S BEEN MY BEST FRIEND FOR FIVE YEARS.

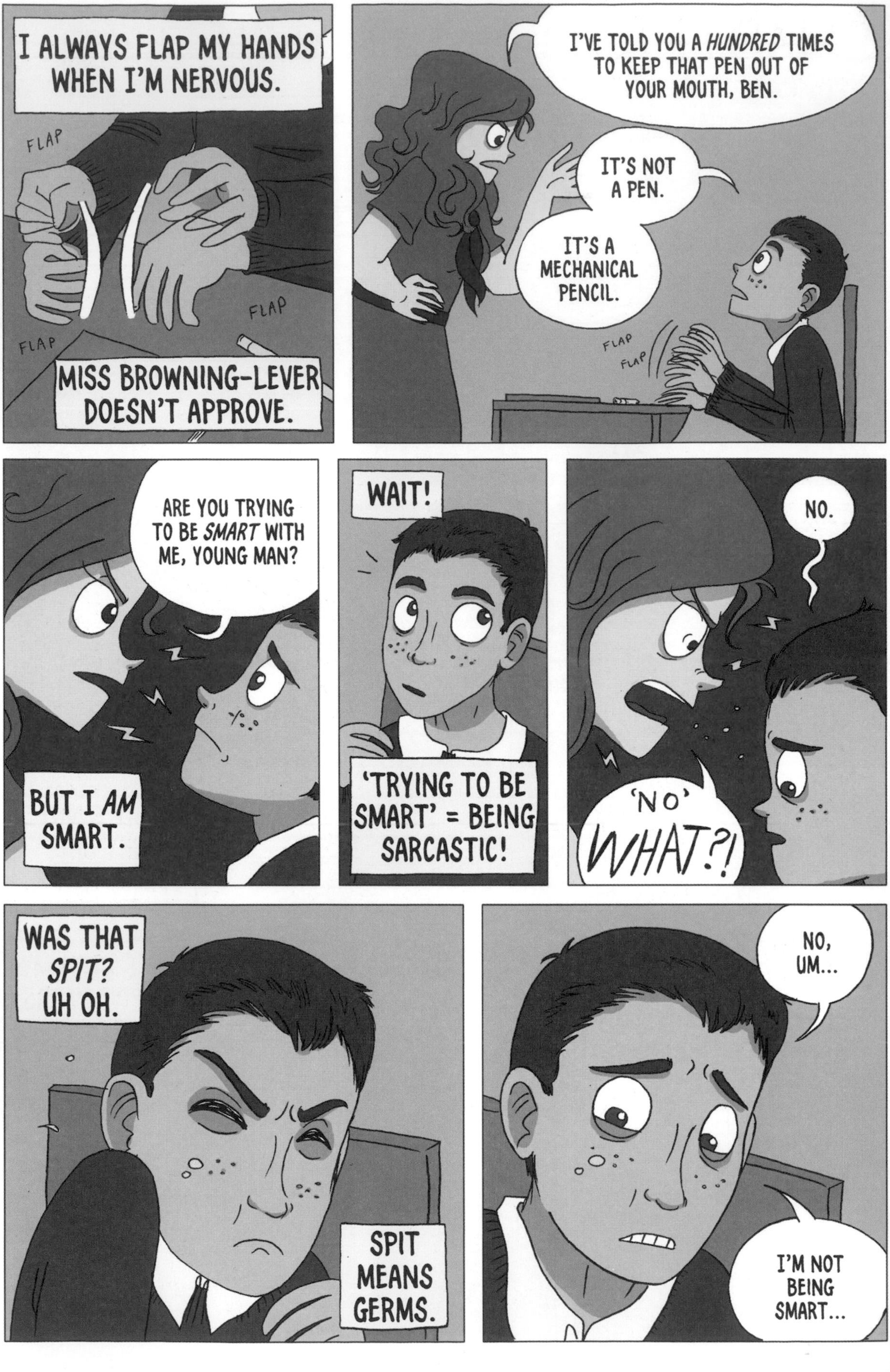

I ALWAYS FLAP MY HANDS WHEN I'M NERVOUS.
FLAP
FLAP
FLAP
MISS BROWNING-LEVER DOESN'T APPROVE.
I'VE TOLD YOU A *HUNDRED* TIMES TO KEEP THAT PEN OUT OF YOUR MOUTH, BEN.
IT'S NOT A PEN.
IT'S A MECHANICAL PENCIL.
FLAP
FLAP
ARE YOU TRYING TO BE *SMART* WITH ME, YOUNG MAN?
BUT I *AM* SMART.
WAIT!
'TRYING TO BE SMART' = BEING SARCASTIC!
NO.
'NO' WHAT?!
WAS THAT *SPIT?* UH OH.
SPIT MEANS GERMS.
NO, UM...
I'M NOT BEING SMART...

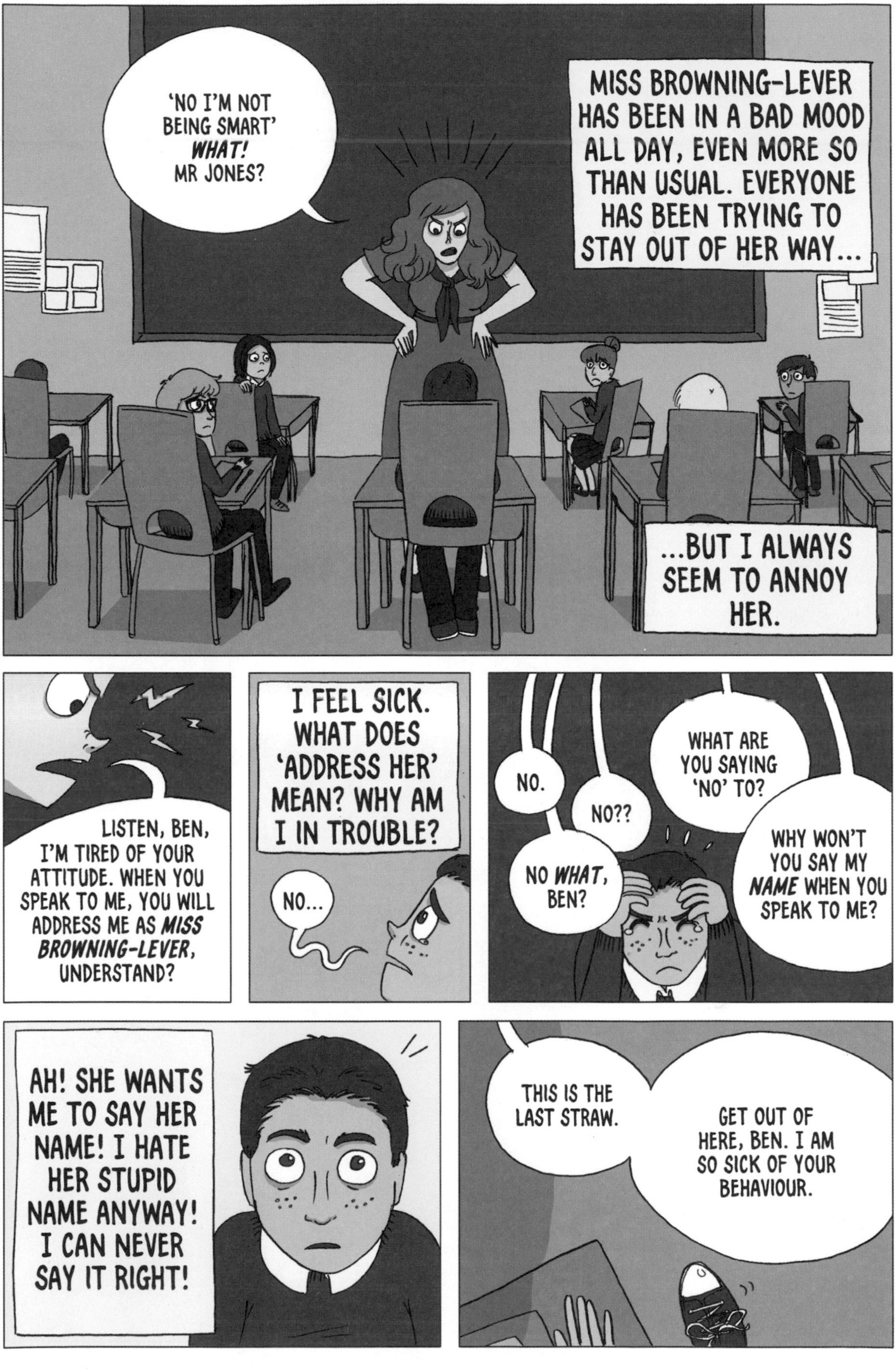
'NO I'M NOT BEING SMART' *WHAT!* MR JONES?
MISS BROWNING-LEVER HAS BEEN IN A BAD MOOD ALL DAY, EVEN MORE SO THAN USUAL. EVERYONE HAS BEEN TRYING TO STAY OUT OF HER WAY...
...BUT I ALWAYS SEEM TO ANNOY HER.
LISTEN, BEN, I'M TIRED OF YOUR ATTITUDE. WHEN YOU SPEAK TO ME, YOU WILL ADDRESS ME AS *MISS BROWNING-LEVER*, UNDERSTAND?
I FEEL SICK. WHAT DOES 'ADDRESS HER' MEAN? WHY AM I IN TROUBLE?
NO...
NO.
NO??
WHAT ARE YOU SAYING 'NO' TO?
NO *WHAT*, BEN?
WHY WON'T YOU SAY MY *NAME* WHEN YOU SPEAK TO ME?
AH! SHE WANTS ME TO SAY HER NAME! I HATE HER STUPID NAME ANYWAY! I CAN NEVER SAY IT RIGHT!
THIS IS THE LAST STRAW.
GET OUT OF HERE, BEN. I AM SO SICK OF YOUR BEHAVIOUR.

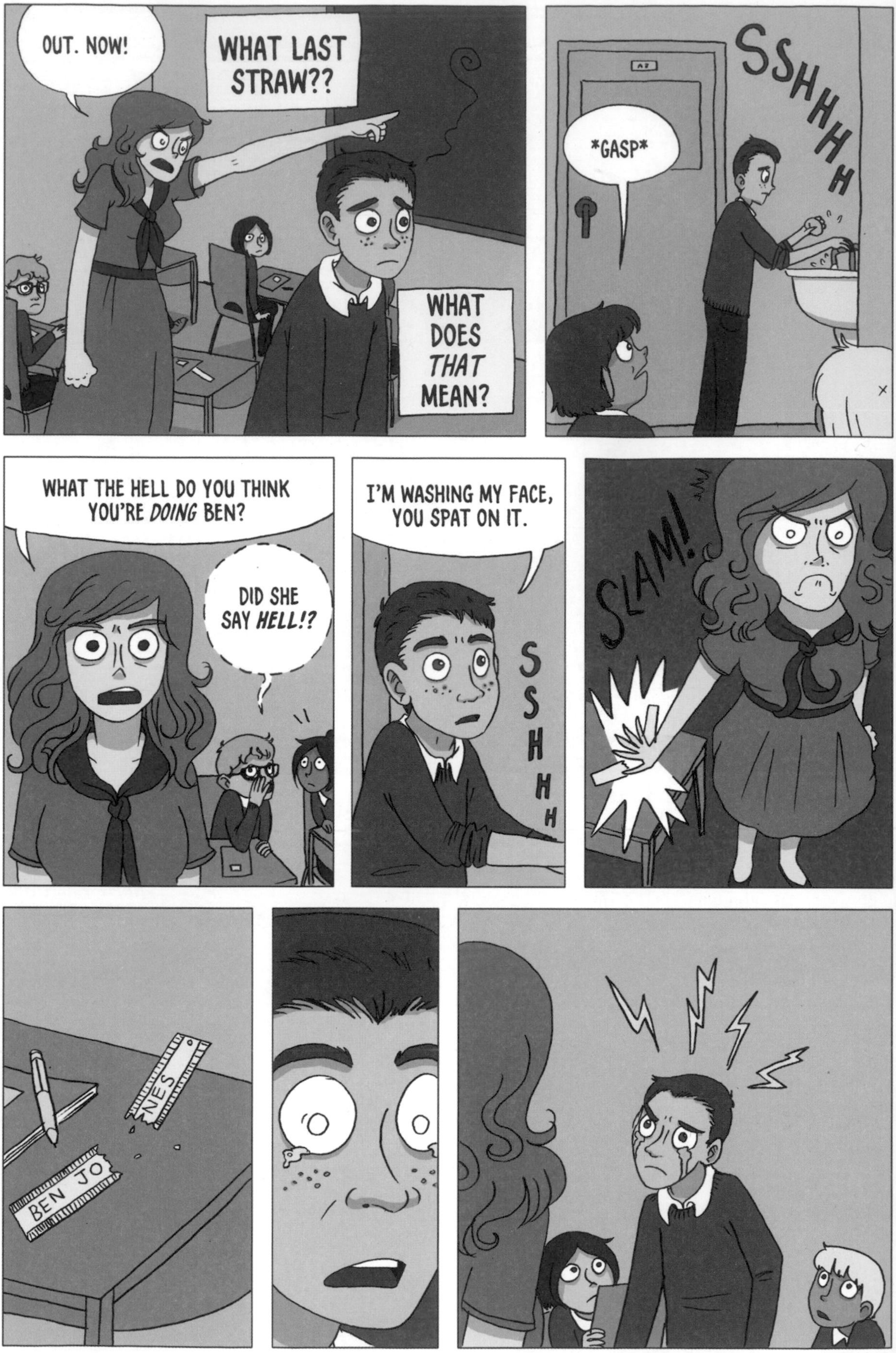
OUT. NOW!
WHAT LAST STRAW??
WHAT DOES *THAT* MEAN?
SSHHHHH
GASP
WHAT THE HELL DO YOU THINK YOU'RE *DOING* BEN?
DID SHE SAY *HELL!?*
I'M WASHING MY FACE, YOU SPAT ON IT.
SSHHH
SLAM!
NES
BEN JO

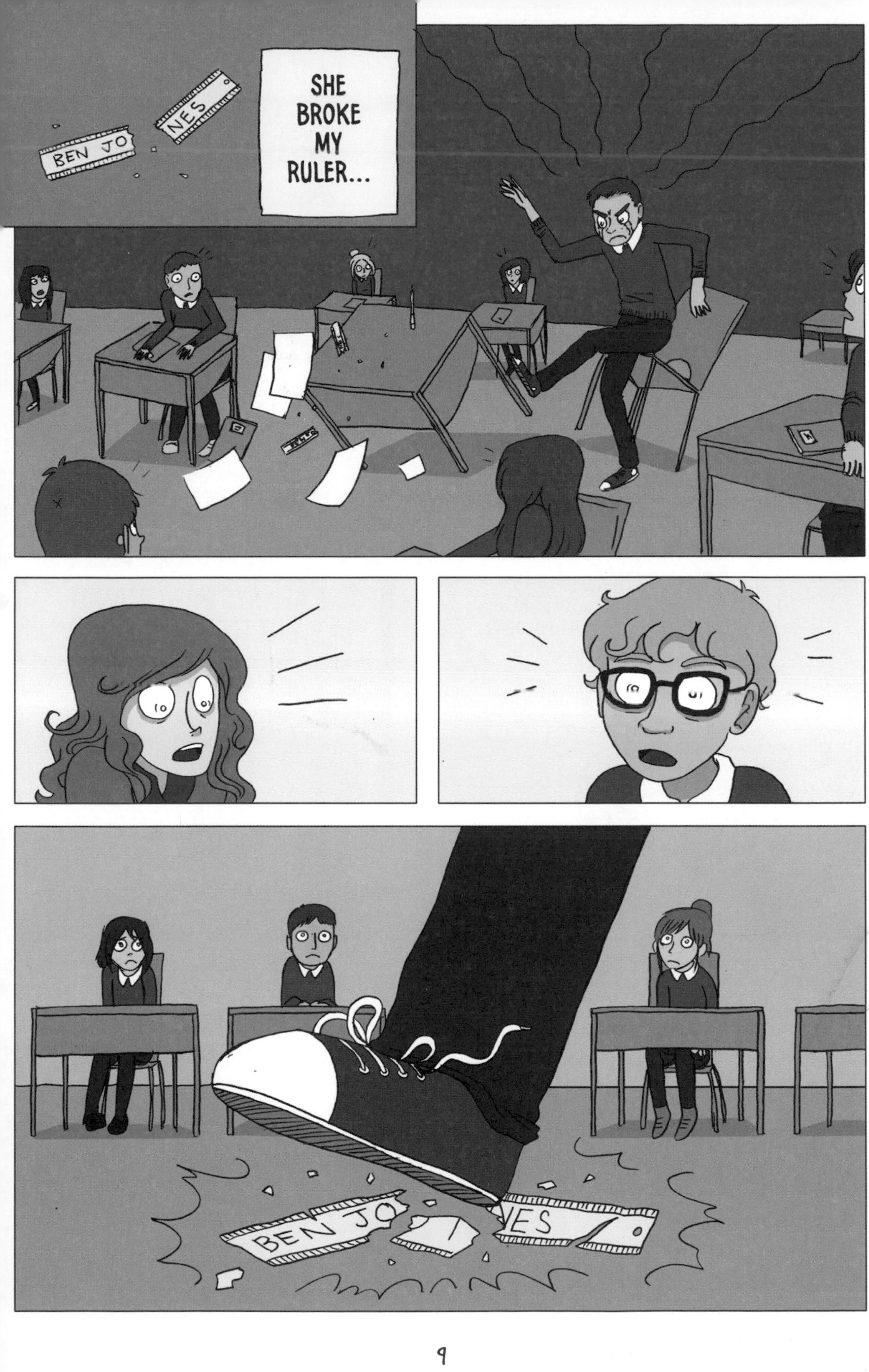
BEN JO
NES
SHE BROKE MY RULER...
BEN JO
ES

CHAPTER 2: THE PLAYGROUND

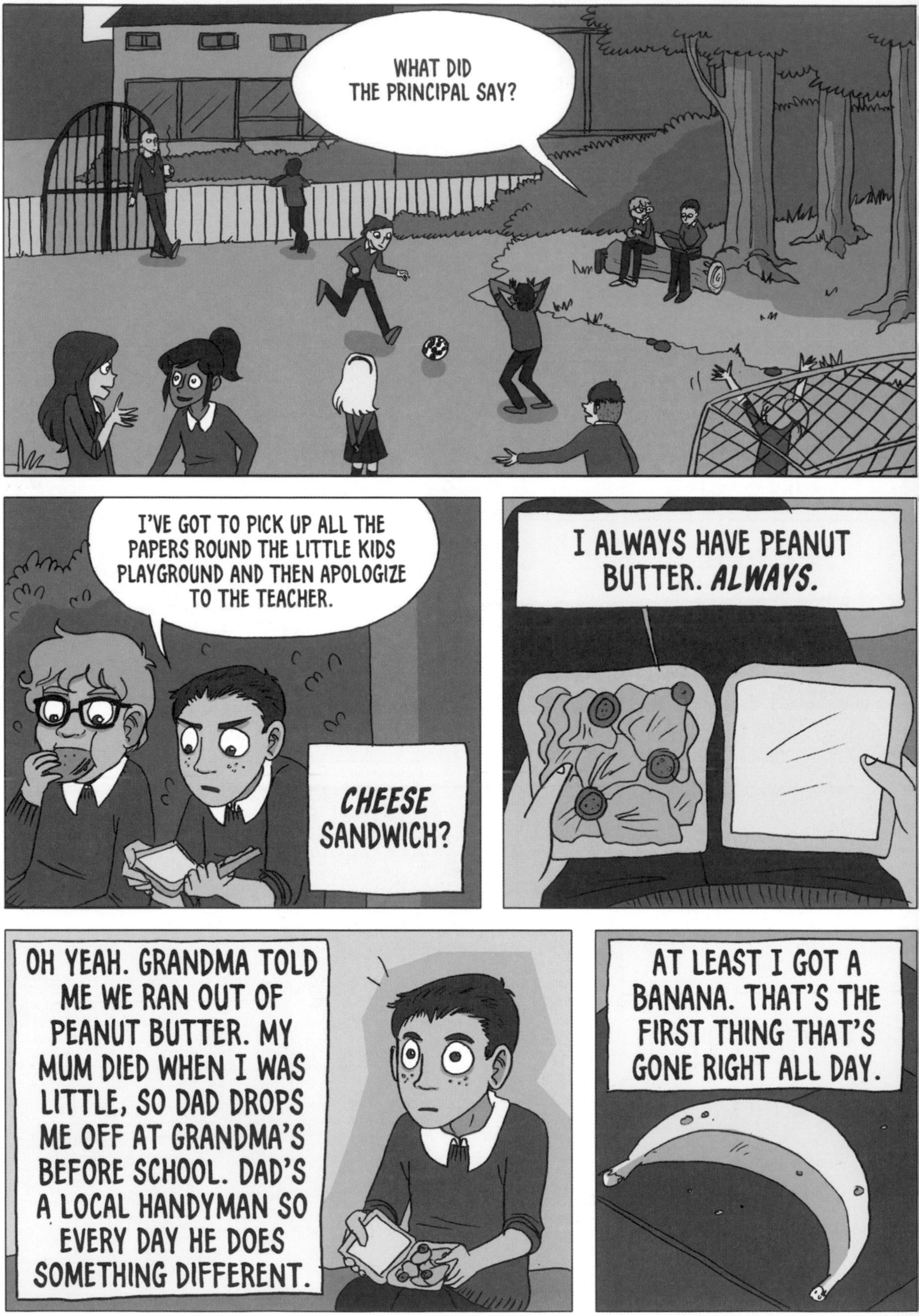
WHAT DID THE PRINCIPAL SAY?
I'VE GOT TO PICK UP ALL THE PAPERS ROUND THE LITTLE KIDS PLAYGROUND AND THEN APOLOGIZE TO THE TEACHER.
CHEESE SANDWICH?
I ALWAYS HAVE PEANUT BUTTER. ALWAYS.
OH YEAH. GRANDMA TOLD ME WE RAN OUT OF PEANUT BUTTER. MY MUM DIED WHEN I WAS LITTLE, SO DAD DROPS ME OFF AT GRANDMA'S BEFORE SCHOOL. DAD'S A LOCAL HANDYMAN SO EVERY DAY HE DOES SOMETHING DIFFERENT.
AT LEAST I GOT A BANANA. THAT'S THE FIRST THING THAT'S GONE RIGHT ALL DAY.

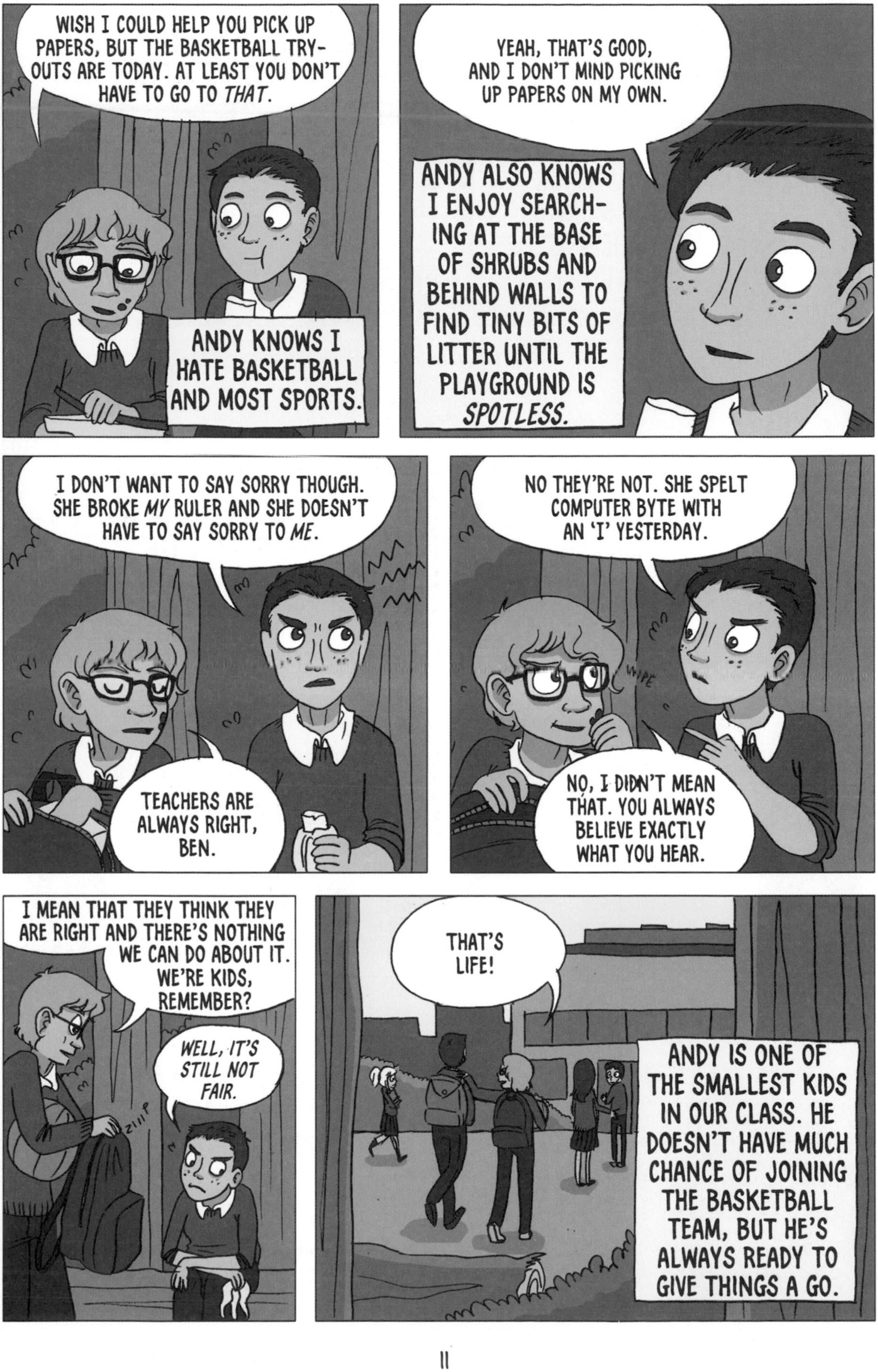
WISH I COULD HELP YOU PICK UP PAPERS, BUT THE BASKETBALL TRY-OUTS ARE TODAY. AT LEAST YOU DON'T HAVE TO GO TO *THAT*.
ANDY KNOWS I HATE BASKETBALL AND MOST SPORTS.
YEAH, THAT'S GOOD, AND I DON'T MIND PICKING UP PAPERS ON MY OWN.
ANDY ALSO KNOWS I ENJOY SEARCHING AT THE BASE OF SHRUBS AND BEHIND WALLS TO FIND TINY BITS OF LITTER UNTIL THE PLAYGROUND IS *SPOTLESS*.
TEACHERS ARE ALWAYS RIGHT, BEN.
I DON'T WANT TO SAY SORRY THOUGH. SHE BROKE *MY* RULER AND SHE DOESN'T HAVE TO SAY SORRY TO *ME*.
NO THEY'RE NOT. SHE SPELT COMPUTER BYTE WITH AN 'I' YESTERDAY.
WIPE
NO, I DIDN'T MEAN THAT. YOU ALWAYS BELIEVE EXACTLY WHAT YOU HEAR.
I MEAN THAT THEY THINK THEY ARE RIGHT AND THERE'S NOTHING WE CAN DO ABOUT IT. WE'RE KIDS, REMEMBER?
WELL, IT'S STILL NOT FAIR.
ZIIIP
THAT'S LIFE!
ANDY IS ONE OF THE SMALLEST KIDS IN OUR CLASS. HE DOESN'T HAVE MUCH CHANCE OF JOINING THE BASKETBALL TEAM, BUT HE'S ALWAYS READY TO GIVE THINGS A GO.

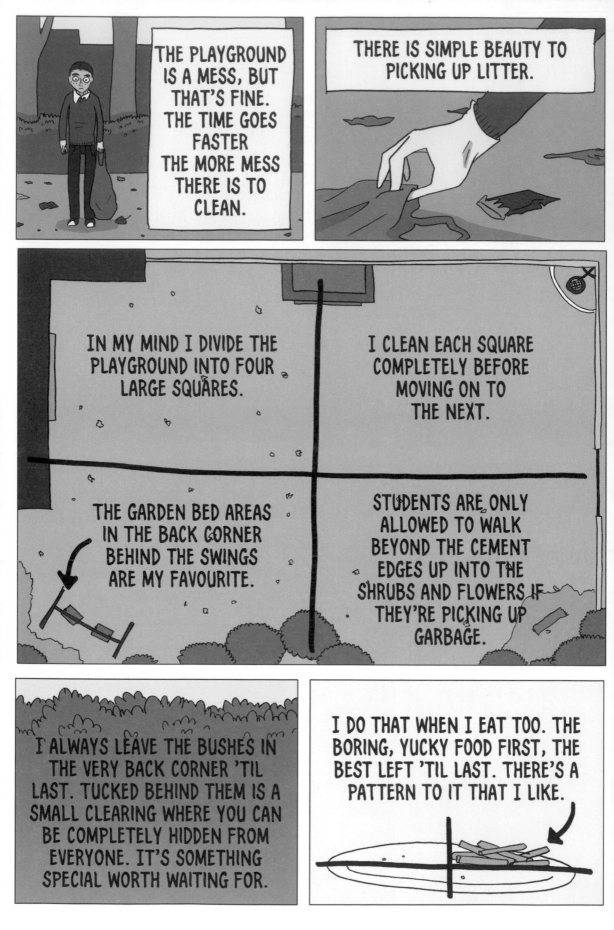

THE PLAYGROUND IS A MESS, BUT THAT'S FINE. THE TIME GOES FASTER THE MORE MESS THERE IS TO CLEAN.

THERE IS SIMPLE BEAUTY TO PICKING UP LITTER.

IN MY MIND I DIVIDE THE PLAYGROUND INTO FOUR LARGE SQUARES.

I CLEAN EACH SQUARE COMPLETELY BEFORE MOVING ON TO THE NEXT.

THE GARDEN BED AREAS IN THE BACK CORNER BEHIND THE SWINGS ARE MY FAVOURITE.

STUDENTS ARE ONLY ALLOWED TO WALK BEYOND THE CEMENT EDGES UP INTO THE SHRUBS AND FLOWERS IF THEY'RE PICKING UP GARBAGE.

I ALWAYS LEAVE THE BUSHES IN THE VERY BACK CORNER 'TIL LAST. TUCKED BEHIND THEM IS A SMALL CLEARING WHERE YOU CAN BE COMPLETELY HIDDEN FROM EVERYONE. IT'S SOMETHING SPECIAL WORTH WAITING FOR.

I DO THAT WHEN I EAT TOO. THE BORING, YUCKY FOOD FIRST, THE BEST LEFT 'TIL LAST. THERE'S A PATTERN TO IT THAT I LIKE.

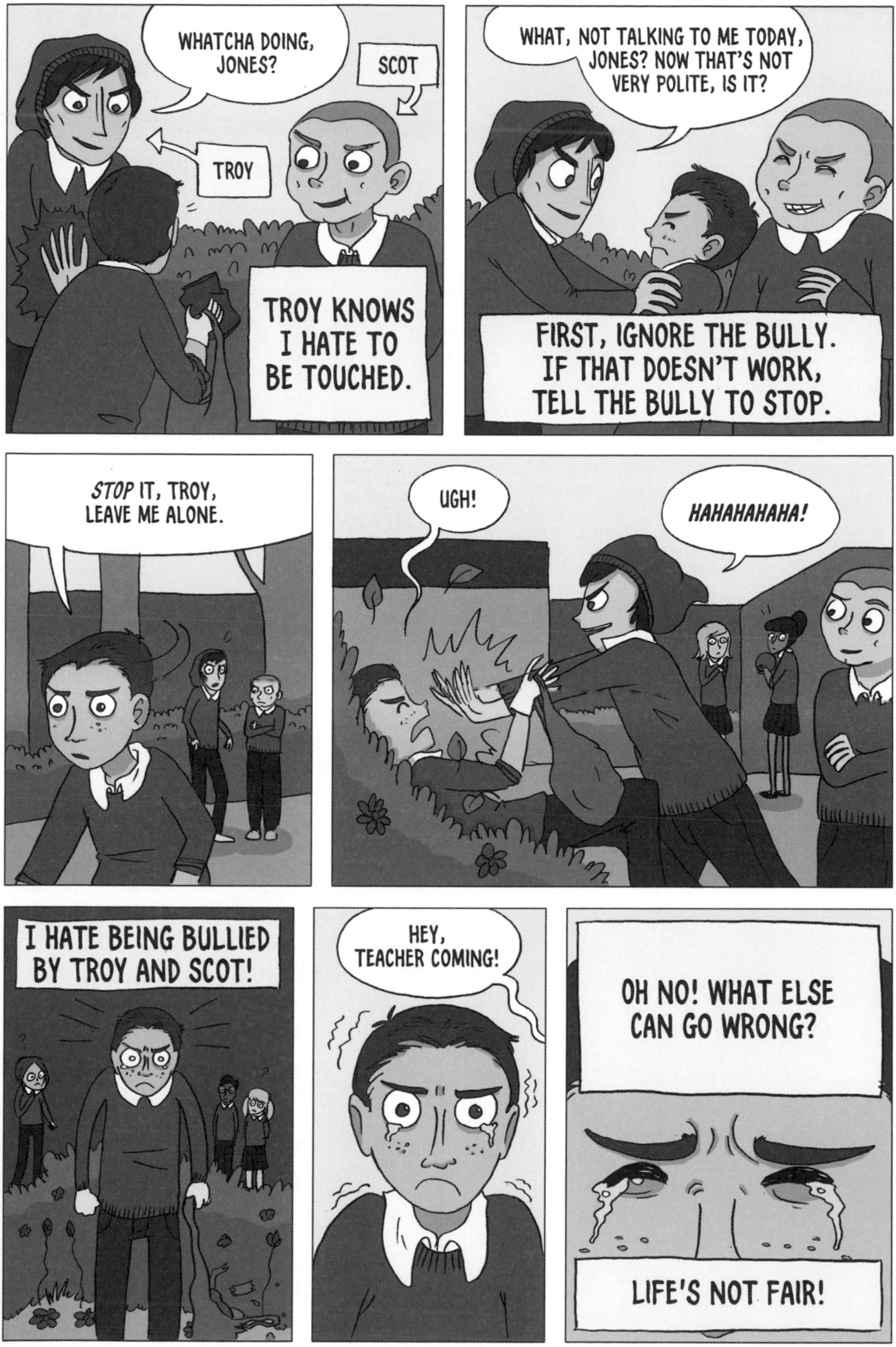
WHATCHA DOING, JONES?
SCOT
TROY
TROY KNOWS I HATE TO BE TOUCHED.
WHAT, NOT TALKING TO ME TODAY, JONES? NOW THAT'S NOT VERY POLITE, IS IT?
FIRST, IGNORE THE BULLY. IF THAT DOESN'T WORK, TELL THE BULLY TO STOP.
STOP IT, TROY, LEAVE ME ALONE.
UGH!
HAHAHAHAHA!
I HATE BEING BULLIED BY TROY AND SCOT!
HEY, TEACHER COMING!
OH NO! WHAT ELSE CAN GO WRONG?
LIFE'S NOT FAIR!

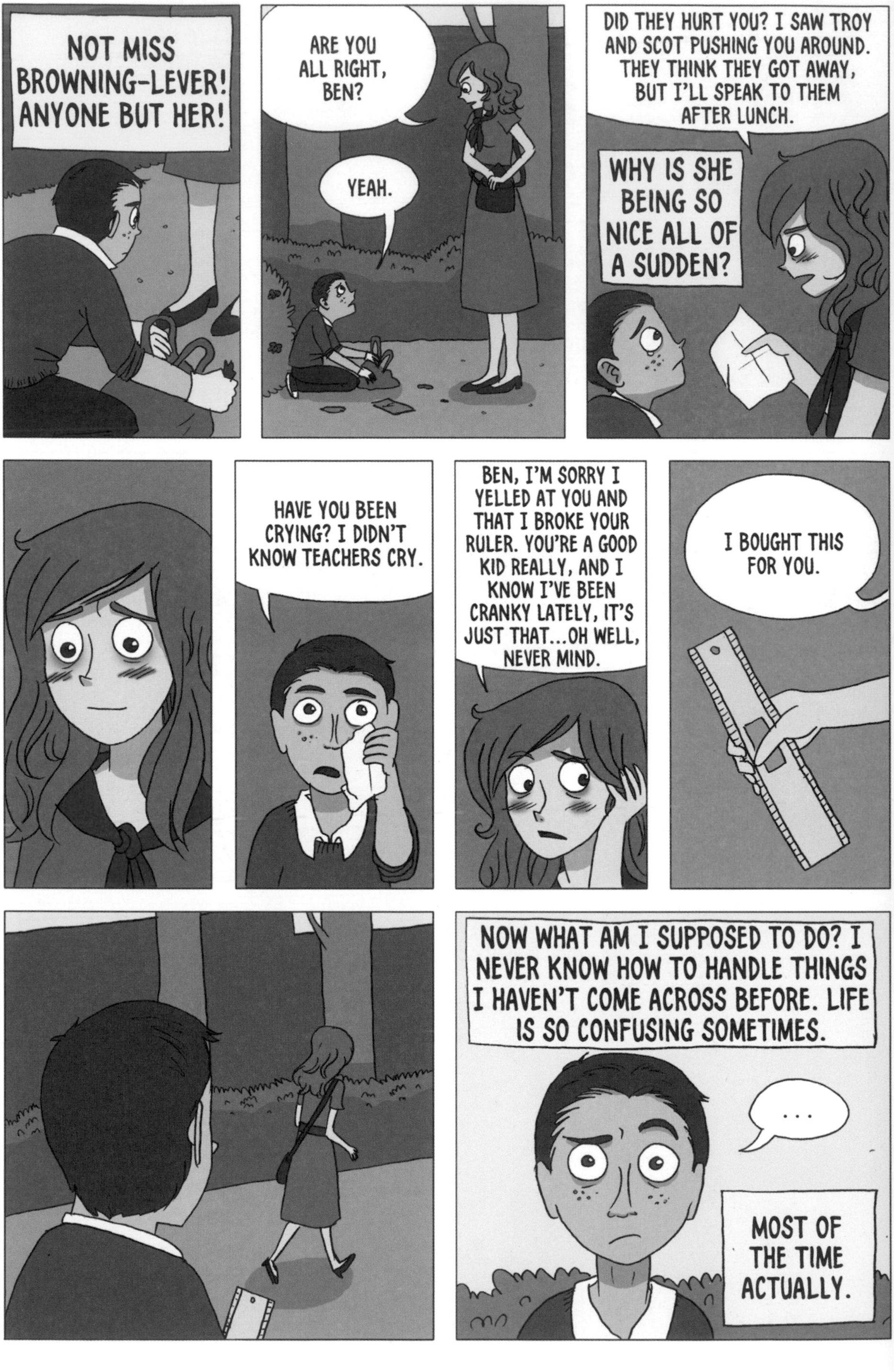
NOT MISS BROWNING-LEVER! ANYONE BUT HER!
ARE YOU ALL RIGHT, BEN?
YEAH.
DID THEY HURT YOU? I SAW TROY AND SCOT PUSHING YOU AROUND. THEY THINK THEY GOT AWAY, BUT I'LL SPEAK TO THEM AFTER LUNCH.
WHY IS SHE BEING SO NICE ALL OF A SUDDEN?
HAVE YOU BEEN CRYING? I DIDN'T KNOW TEACHERS CRY.
BEN, I'M SORRY I YELLED AT YOU AND THAT I BROKE YOUR RULER. YOU'RE A GOOD KID REALLY, AND I KNOW I'VE BEEN CRANKY LATELY, IT'S JUST THAT...OH WELL, NEVER MIND.
I BOUGHT THIS FOR YOU.
NOW WHAT AM I SUPPOSED TO DO? I NEVER KNOW HOW TO HANDLE THINGS I HAVEN'T COME ACROSS BEFORE. LIFE IS SO CONFUSING SOMETIMES.
...
MOST OF THE TIME ACTUALLY.

CHAPTER 3: THE BLUE BOTTLE

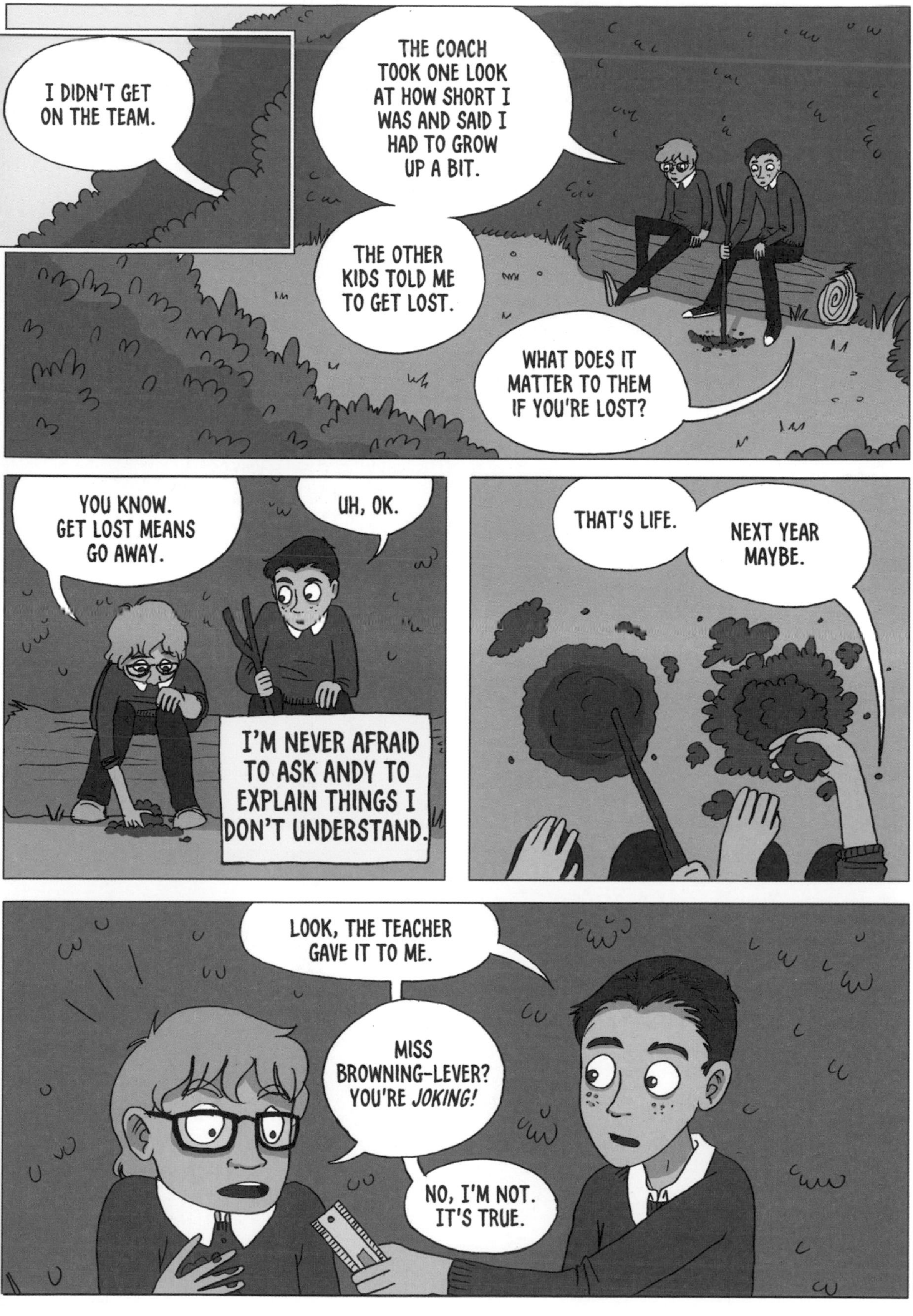

I DIDN'T GET ON THE TEAM.
THE COACH TOOK ONE LOOK AT HOW SHORT I WAS AND SAID I HAD TO GROW UP A BIT.
THE OTHER KIDS TOLD ME TO GET LOST.
WHAT DOES IT MATTER TO THEM IF YOU'RE LOST?
YOU KNOW. GET LOST MEANS GO AWAY.
UH, OK.
I'M NEVER AFRAID TO ASK ANDY TO EXPLAIN THINGS I DON'T UNDERSTAND.
THAT'S LIFE.
NEXT YEAR MAYBE.
LOOK, THE TEACHER GAVE IT TO ME.
MISS BROWNING-LEVER? YOU'RE *JOKING!*
NO, I'M NOT. IT'S TRUE.

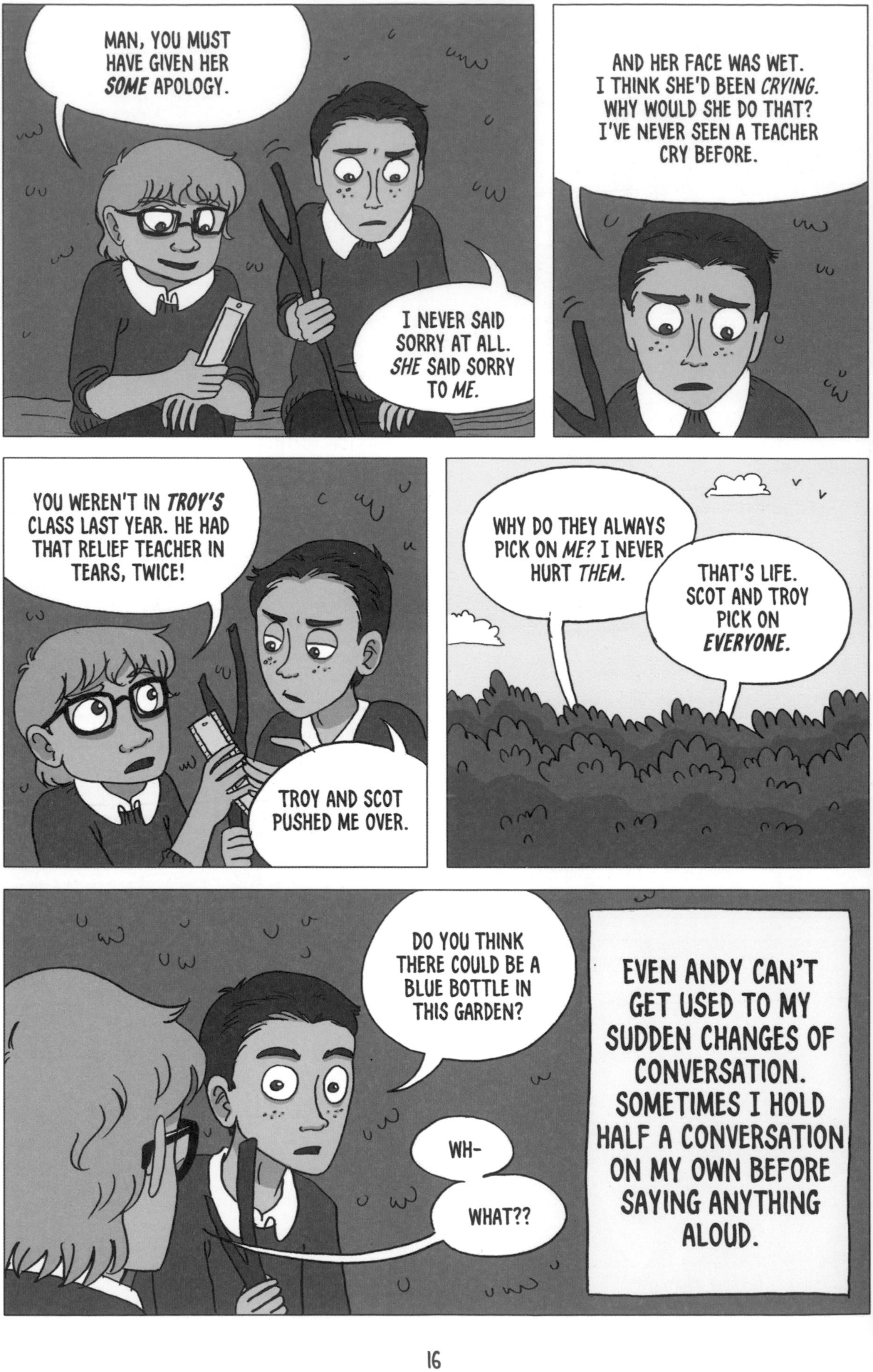
MAN, YOU MUST HAVE GIVEN HER *SOME* APOLOGY.
I NEVER SAID SORRY AT ALL. *SHE* SAID SORRY TO *ME*.
AND HER FACE WAS WET. I THINK SHE'D BEEN *CRYING*. WHY WOULD SHE DO THAT? I'VE NEVER SEEN A TEACHER CRY BEFORE.
YOU WEREN'T IN *TROY'S* CLASS LAST YEAR. HE HAD THAT RELIEF TEACHER IN TEARS, TWICE!
TROY AND SCOT PUSHED ME OVER.
WHY DO THEY ALWAYS PICK ON *ME?* I NEVER HURT *THEM*.
THAT'S LIFE. SCOT AND TROY PICK ON *EVERYONE*.
DO YOU THINK THERE COULD BE A BLUE BOTTLE IN THIS GARDEN?
WH-
WHAT??
EVEN ANDY CAN'T GET USED TO MY SUDDEN CHANGES OF CONVERSATION. SOMETIMES I HOLD HALF A CONVERSATION ON MY OWN BEFORE SAYING ANYTHING ALOUD.

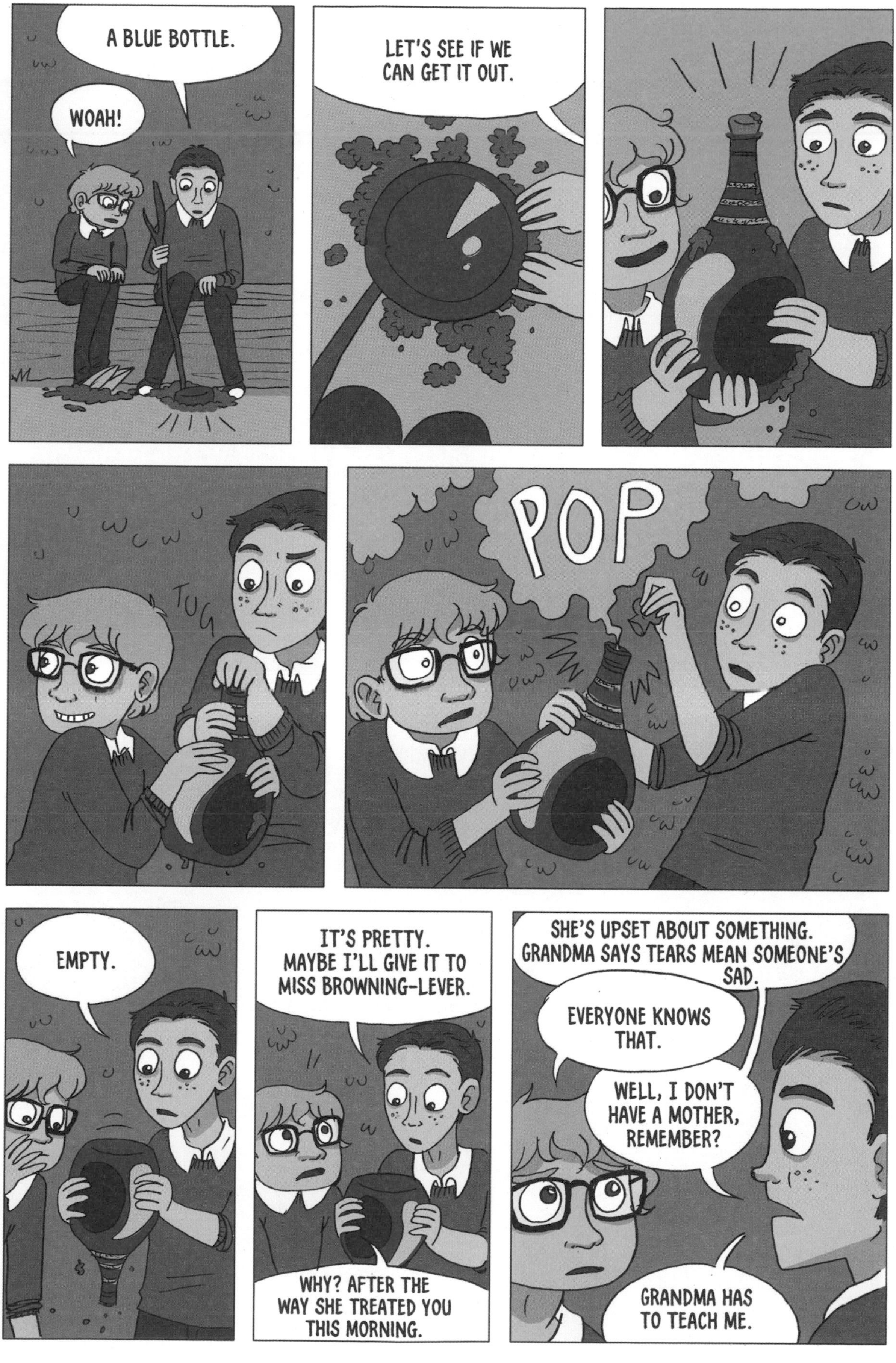
A BLUE BOTTLE.
WOAH!
LET'S SEE IF WE CAN GET IT OUT.
TUG
POP
EMPTY.
IT'S PRETTY. MAYBE I'LL GIVE IT TO MISS BROWNING-LEVER.
WHY? AFTER THE WAY SHE TREATED YOU THIS MORNING.
SHE'S UPSET ABOUT SOMETHING. GRANDMA SAYS TEARS MEAN SOMEONE'S SAD.
EVERYONE KNOWS THAT.
WELL, I DON'T HAVE A MOTHER, REMEMBER?
GRANDMA HAS TO TEACH ME.

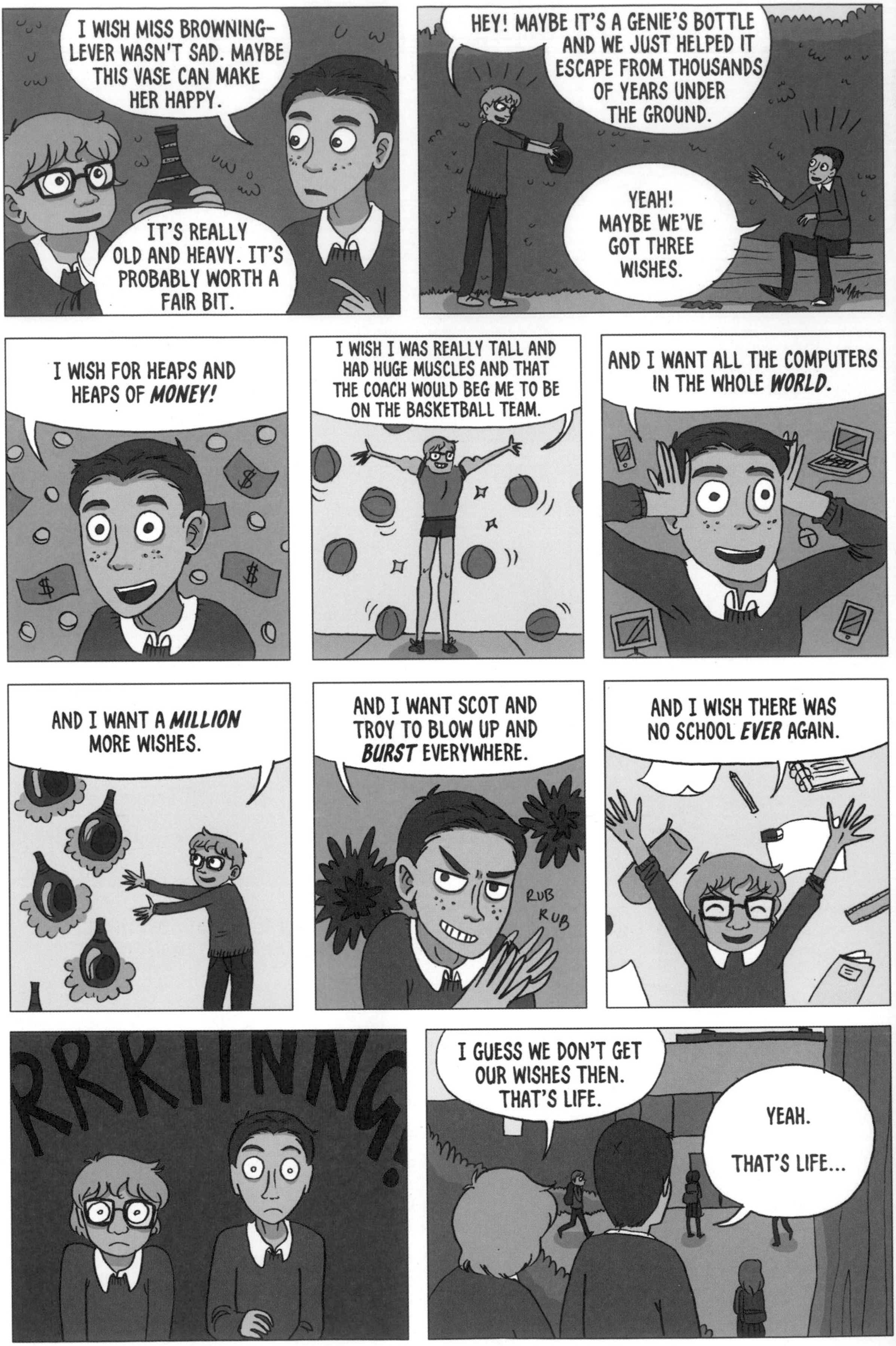
I WISH MISS BROWNING-LEVER WASN'T SAD. MAYBE THIS VASE CAN MAKE HER HAPPY.
IT'S REALLY OLD AND HEAVY. IT'S PROBABLY WORTH A FAIR BIT.
HEY! MAYBE IT'S A GENIE'S BOTTLE AND WE JUST HELPED IT ESCAPE FROM THOUSANDS OF YEARS UNDER THE GROUND.
YEAH! MAYBE WE'VE GOT THREE WISHES.
I WISH FOR HEAPS AND HEAPS OF *MONEY!*
I WISH I WAS REALLY TALL AND HAD HUGE MUSCLES AND THAT THE COACH WOULD BEG ME TO BE ON THE BASKETBALL TEAM.
AND I WANT ALL THE COMPUTERS IN THE WHOLE *WORLD.*
AND I WANT A *MILLION* MORE WISHES.
AND I WANT SCOT AND TROY TO BLOW UP AND *BURST* EVERYWHERE.
RUB
RUB
AND I WISH THERE WAS NO SCHOOL *EVER* AGAIN.
RRRIINNG!
I GUESS WE DON'T GET OUR WISHES THEN. THAT'S LIFE.
YEAH.
THAT'S LIFE...

CHAPTER 4: FRIDAY NIGHT

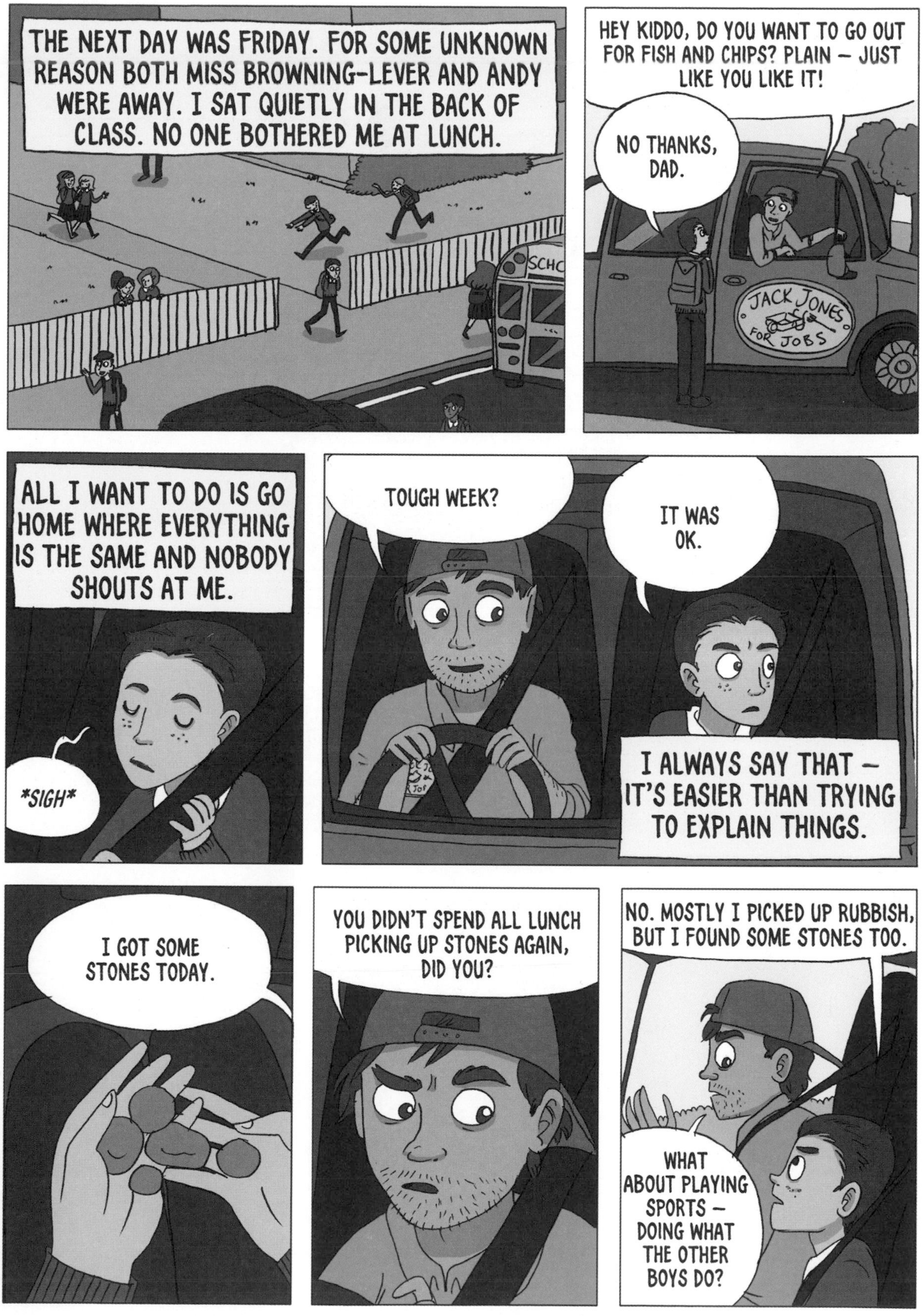
THE NEXT DAY WAS FRIDAY. FOR SOME UNKNOWN REASON BOTH MISS BROWNING-LEVER AND ANDY WERE AWAY. I SAT QUIETLY IN THE BACK OF CLASS. NO ONE BOTHERED ME AT LUNCH.
SCHO
HEY KIDDO, DO YOU WANT TO GO OUT FOR FISH AND CHIPS? PLAIN – JUST LIKE YOU LIKE IT!
NO THANKS, DAD.
JACK JONES FOR JOBS
ALL I WANT TO DO IS GO HOME WHERE EVERYTHING IS THE SAME AND NOBODY SHOUTS AT ME.
SIGH
TOUGH WEEK?
IT WAS OK.
I ALWAYS SAY THAT – IT'S EASIER THAN TRYING TO EXPLAIN THINGS.
I GOT SOME STONES TODAY.
YOU DIDN'T SPEND ALL LUNCH PICKING UP STONES AGAIN, DID YOU?
NO. MOSTLY I PICKED UP RUBBISH, BUT I FOUND SOME STONES TOO.
WHAT ABOUT PLAYING SPORTS – DOING WHAT THE OTHER BOYS DO?

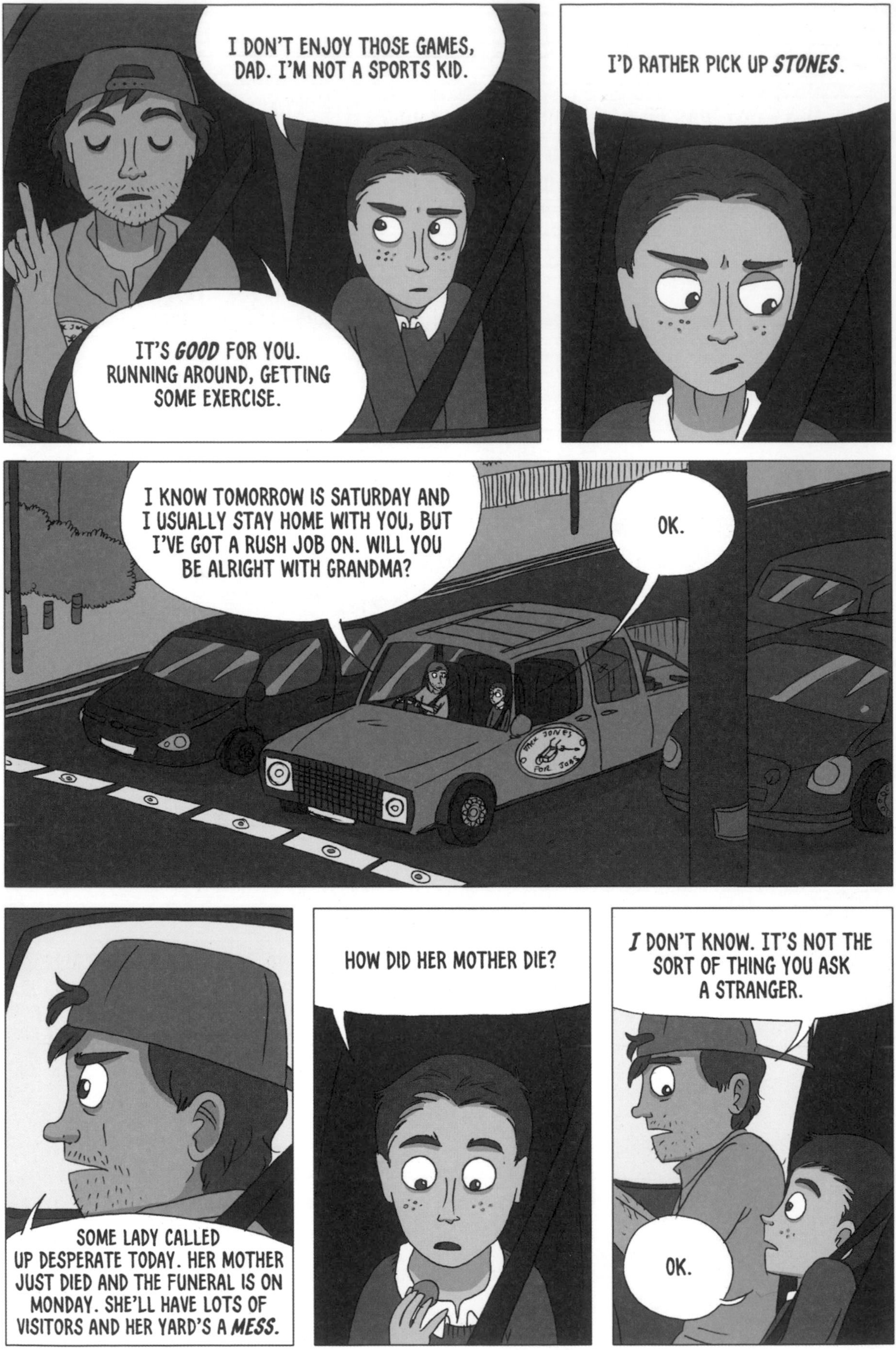

I DON'T ENJOY THOSE GAMES, DAD. I'M NOT A SPORTS KID.
IT'S *GOOD* FOR YOU. RUNNING AROUND, GETTING SOME EXERCISE.
I'D RATHER PICK UP *STONES*.
I KNOW TOMORROW IS SATURDAY AND I USUALLY STAY HOME WITH YOU, BUT I'VE GOT A RUSH JOB ON. WILL YOU BE ALRIGHT WITH GRANDMA?
OK.
SOME LADY CALLED UP DESPERATE TODAY. HER MOTHER JUST DIED AND THE FUNERAL IS ON MONDAY. SHE'LL HAVE LOTS OF VISITORS AND HER YARD'S A *MESS*.
HOW DID HER MOTHER DIE?
I DON'T KNOW. IT'S NOT THE SORT OF THING YOU ASK A STRANGER.
OK.

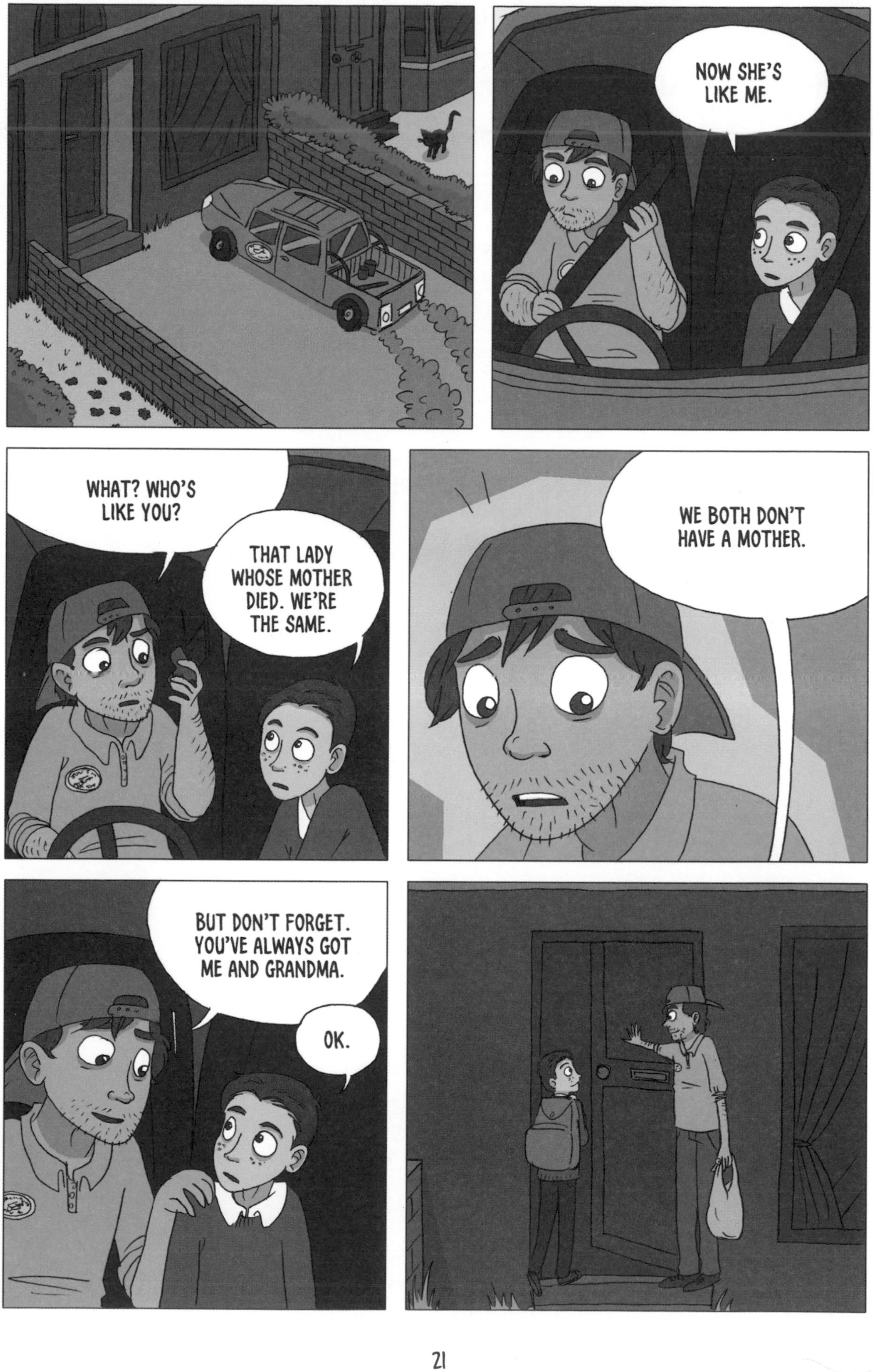
NOW SHE'S LIKE ME.
WHAT? WHO'S LIKE YOU?
THAT LADY WHOSE MOTHER DIED. WE'RE THE SAME.
WE BOTH DON'T HAVE A MOTHER.
BUT DON'T FORGET. YOU'VE ALWAYS GOT ME AND GRANDMA.
OK.

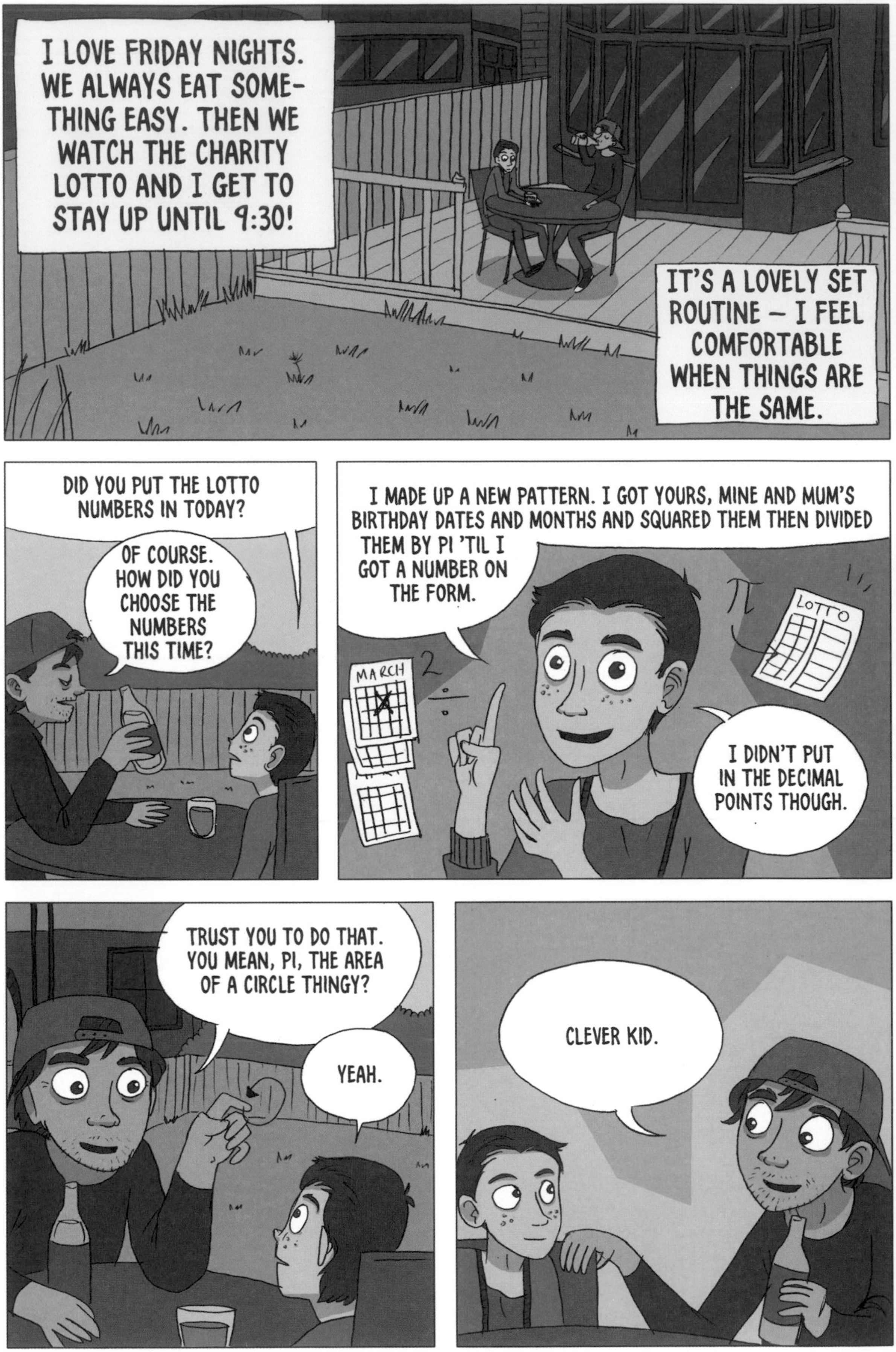
I LOVE FRIDAY NIGHTS. WE ALWAYS EAT SOME-THING EASY. THEN WE WATCH THE CHARITY LOTTO AND I GET TO STAY UP UNTIL 9:30!
IT'S A LOVELY SET ROUTINE – I FEEL COMFORTABLE WHEN THINGS ARE THE SAME.
DID YOU PUT THE LOTTO NUMBERS IN TODAY?
OF COURSE. HOW DID YOU CHOOSE THE NUMBERS THIS TIME?
I MADE UP A NEW PATTERN. I GOT YOURS, MINE AND MUM'S BIRTHDAY DATES AND MONTHS AND SQUARED THEM THEN DIVIDED THEM BY PI 'TIL I GOT A NUMBER ON THE FORM.
MARCH
LOTTO
I DIDN'T PUT IN THE DECIMAL POINTS THOUGH.
TRUST YOU TO DO THAT. YOU MEAN, PI, THE AREA OF A CIRCLE THINGY?
YEAH.
CLEVER KID.

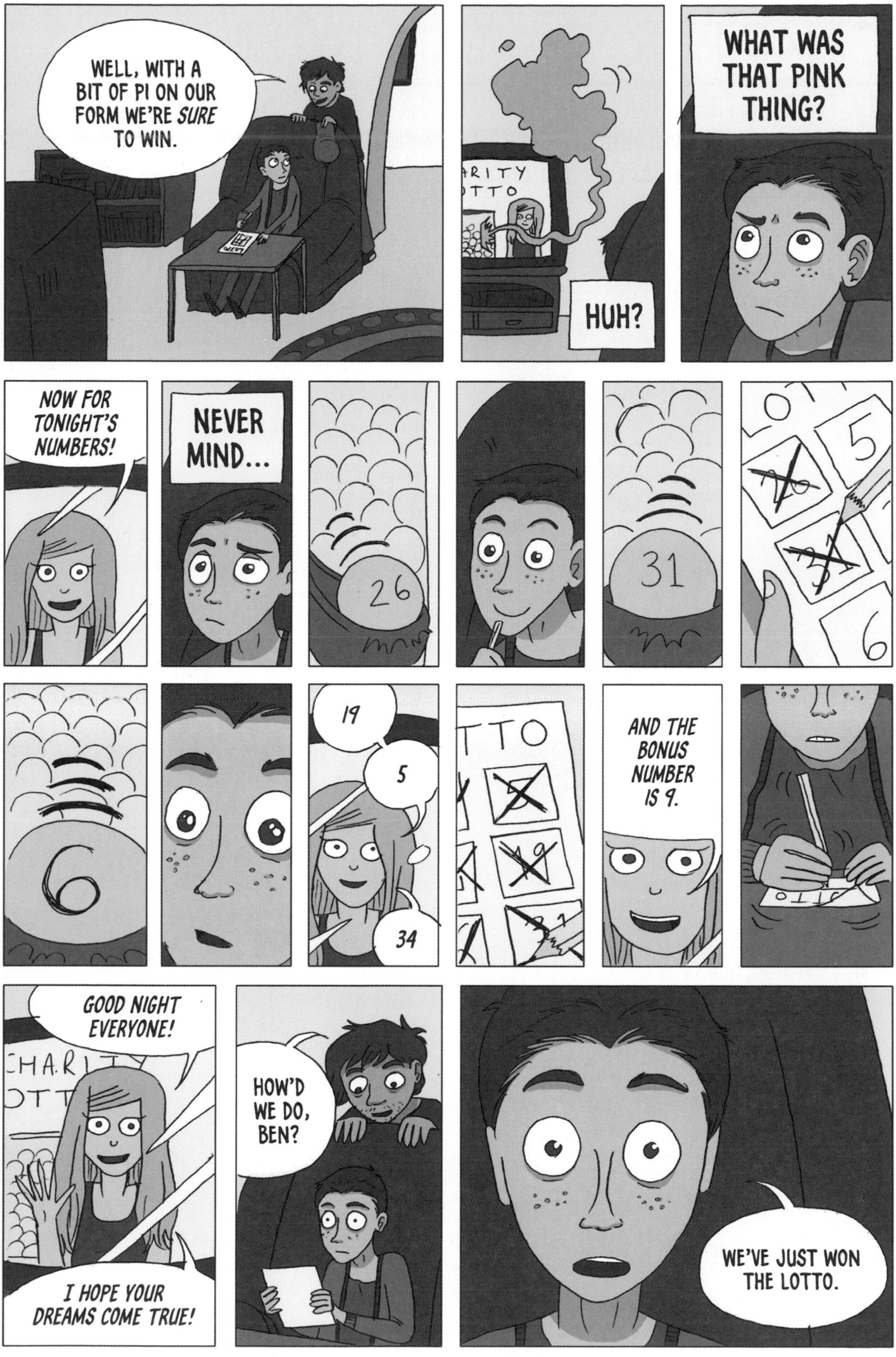
WELL, WITH A BIT OF PI ON OUR FORM WE'RE *SURE* TO WIN.
CHARITY LOTTO
HUH?
WHAT WAS THAT PINK THING?
NOW FOR TONIGHT'S NUMBERS!
NEVER MIND...
26
31
6
19
5
34
AND THE BONUS NUMBER IS 9.
GOOD NIGHT EVERYONE!
I HOPE YOUR DREAMS COME TRUE!
HOW'D WE DO, BEN?
WE'VE JUST WON THE LOTTO.

CHAPTER 5: WHAT TO BUY

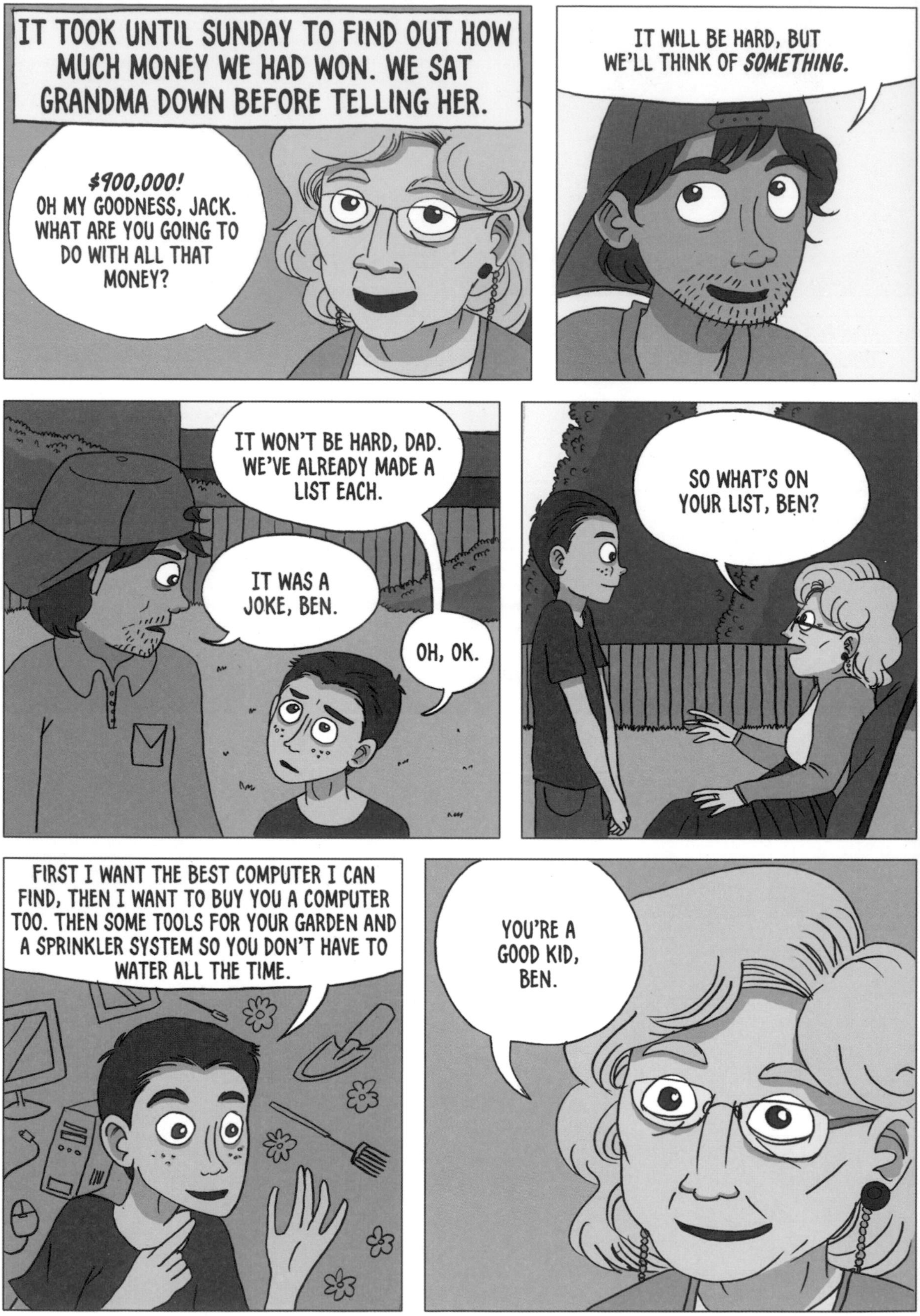
IT TOOK UNTIL SUNDAY TO FIND OUT HOW MUCH MONEY WE HAD WON. WE SAT GRANDMA DOWN BEFORE TELLING HER.
$900,000! OH MY GOODNESS, JACK. WHAT ARE YOU GOING TO DO WITH ALL THAT MONEY?
IT WILL BE HARD, BUT WE'LL THINK OF SOMETHING.
IT WON'T BE HARD, DAD. WE'VE ALREADY MADE A LIST EACH.
IT WAS A JOKE, BEN.
OH, OK.
SO WHAT'S ON YOUR LIST, BEN?
FIRST I WANT THE BEST COMPUTER I CAN FIND, THEN I WANT TO BUY YOU A COMPUTER TOO. THEN SOME TOOLS FOR YOUR GARDEN AND A SPRINKLER SYSTEM SO YOU DON'T HAVE TO WATER ALL THE TIME.
YOU'RE A GOOD KID, BEN.

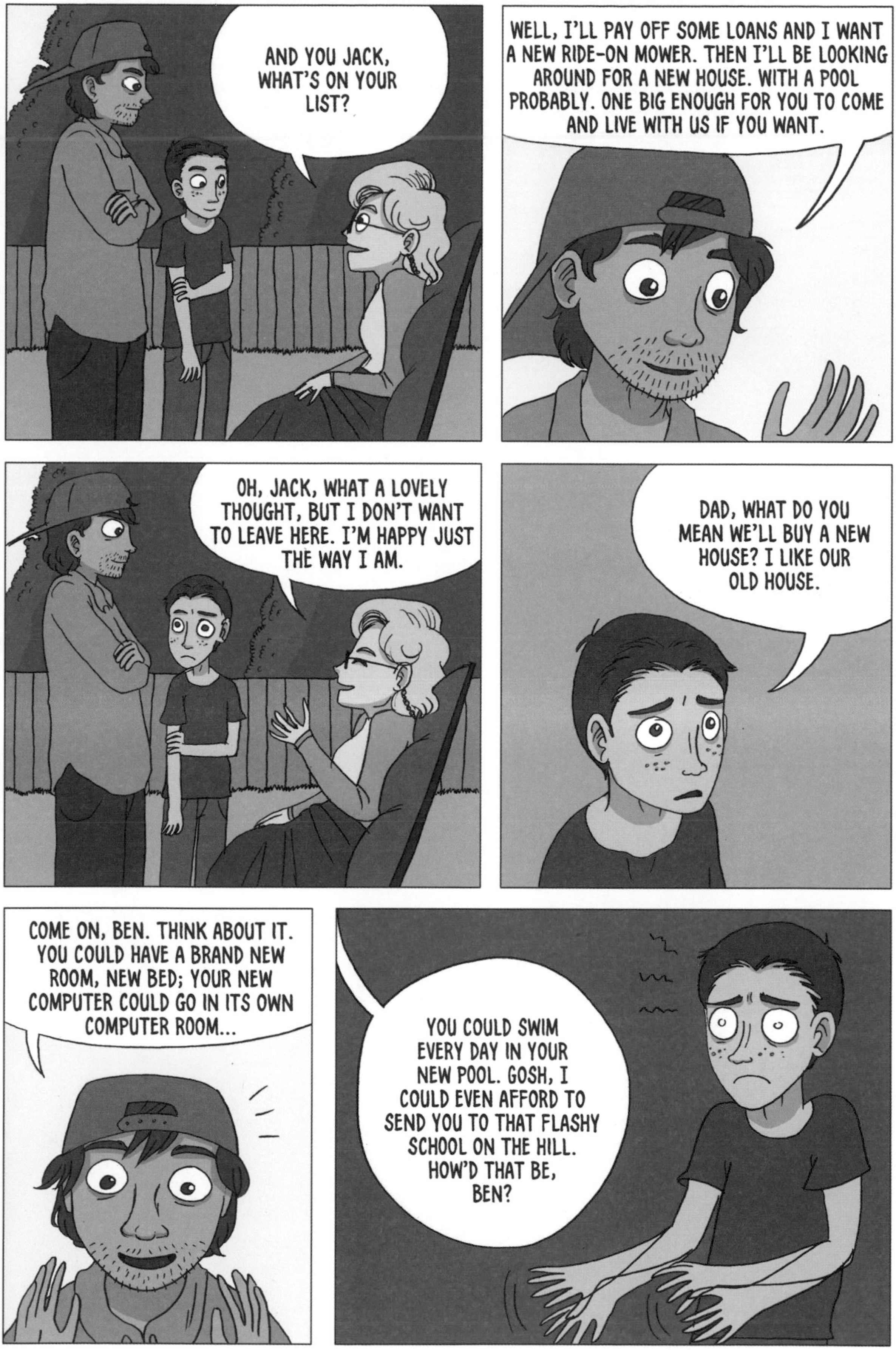
AND YOU JACK, WHAT'S ON YOUR LIST?
WELL, I'LL PAY OFF SOME LOANS AND I WANT A NEW RIDE-ON MOWER. THEN I'LL BE LOOKING AROUND FOR A NEW HOUSE. WITH A POOL PROBABLY. ONE BIG ENOUGH FOR YOU TO COME AND LIVE WITH US IF YOU WANT.
OH, JACK, WHAT A LOVELY THOUGHT, BUT I DON'T WANT TO LEAVE HERE. I'M HAPPY JUST THE WAY I AM.
DAD, WHAT DO YOU MEAN WE'LL BUY A NEW HOUSE? I LIKE OUR OLD HOUSE.
COME ON, BEN. THINK ABOUT IT. YOU COULD HAVE A BRAND NEW ROOM, NEW BED; YOUR NEW COMPUTER COULD GO IN ITS OWN COMPUTER ROOM...
YOU COULD SWIM EVERY DAY IN YOUR NEW POOL. GOSH, I COULD EVEN AFFORD TO SEND YOU TO THAT FLASHY SCHOOL ON THE HILL. HOW'D THAT BE, BEN?

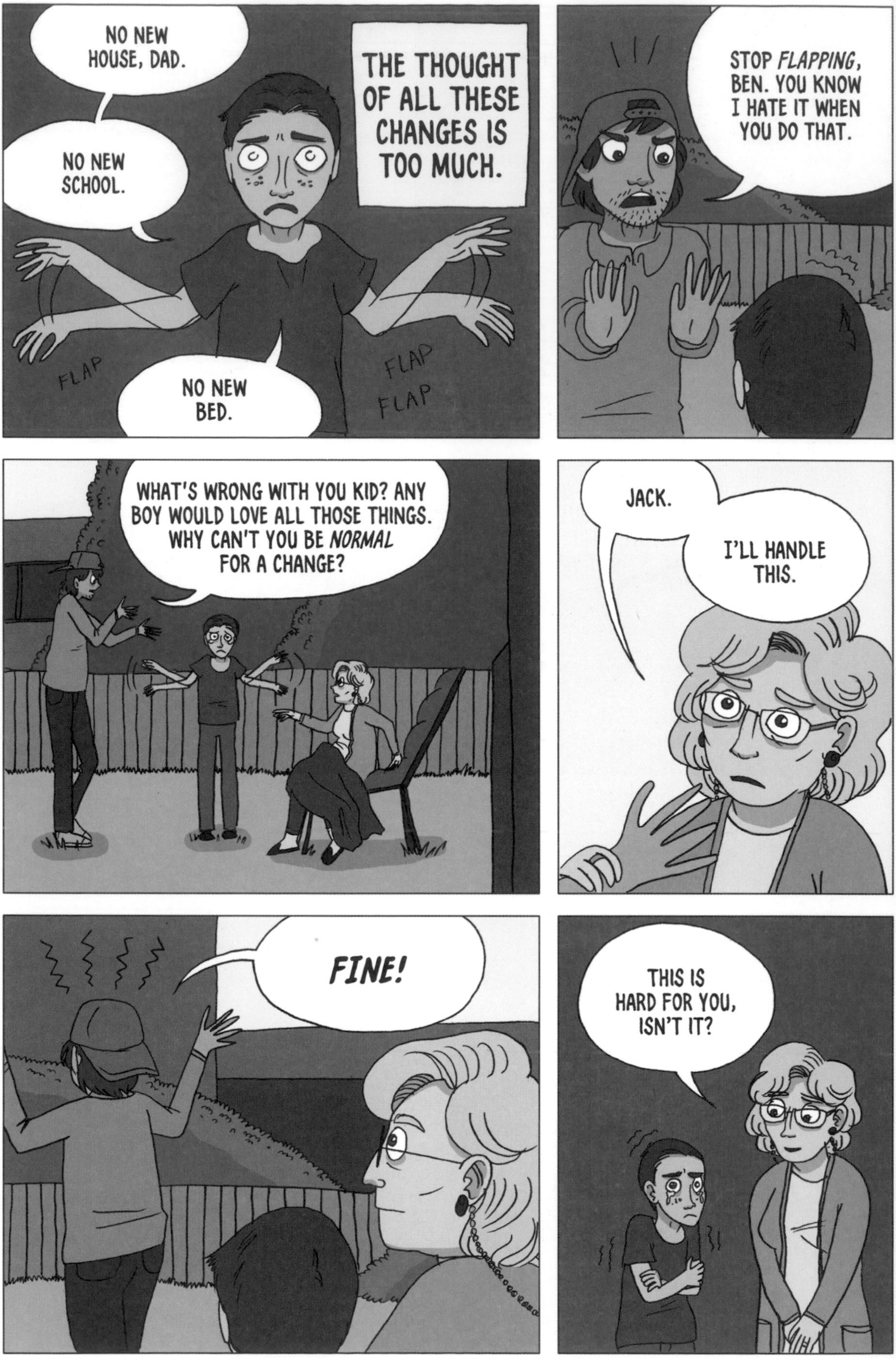
NO NEW HOUSE, DAD.
NO NEW SCHOOL.
THE THOUGHT OF ALL THESE CHANGES IS TOO MUCH.
FLAP
NO NEW BED.
FLAP FLAP
STOP *FLAPPING*, BEN. YOU KNOW I HATE IT WHEN YOU DO THAT.
WHAT'S WRONG WITH YOU KID? ANY BOY WOULD LOVE ALL THOSE THINGS. WHY CAN'T YOU BE *NORMAL* FOR A CHANGE?
JACK.
I'LL HANDLE THIS.
FINE!
THIS IS HARD FOR YOU, ISN'T IT?

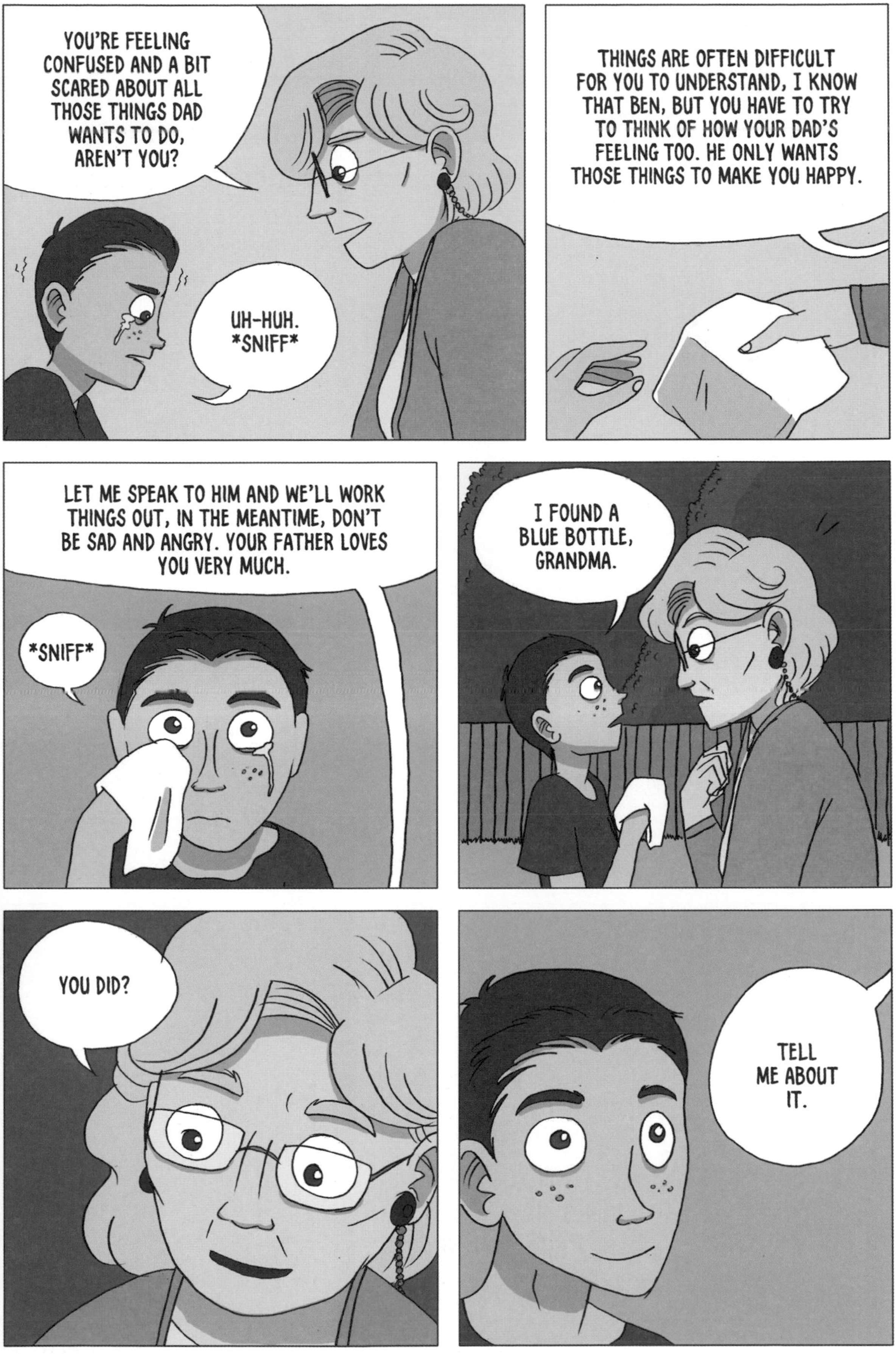
YOU'RE FEELING CONFUSED AND A BIT SCARED ABOUT ALL THOSE THINGS DAD WANTS TO DO, AREN'T YOU?
UH-HUH. *SNIFF*
THINGS ARE OFTEN DIFFICULT FOR YOU TO UNDERSTAND, I KNOW THAT BEN, BUT YOU HAVE TO TRY TO THINK OF HOW YOUR DAD'S FEELING TOO. HE ONLY WANTS THOSE THINGS TO MAKE YOU HAPPY.
LET ME SPEAK TO HIM AND WE'LL WORK THINGS OUT, IN THE MEANTIME, DON'T BE SAD AND ANGRY. YOUR FATHER LOVES YOU VERY MUCH.
SNIFF
I FOUND A BLUE BOTTLE, GRANDMA.
YOU DID?
TELL ME ABOUT IT.

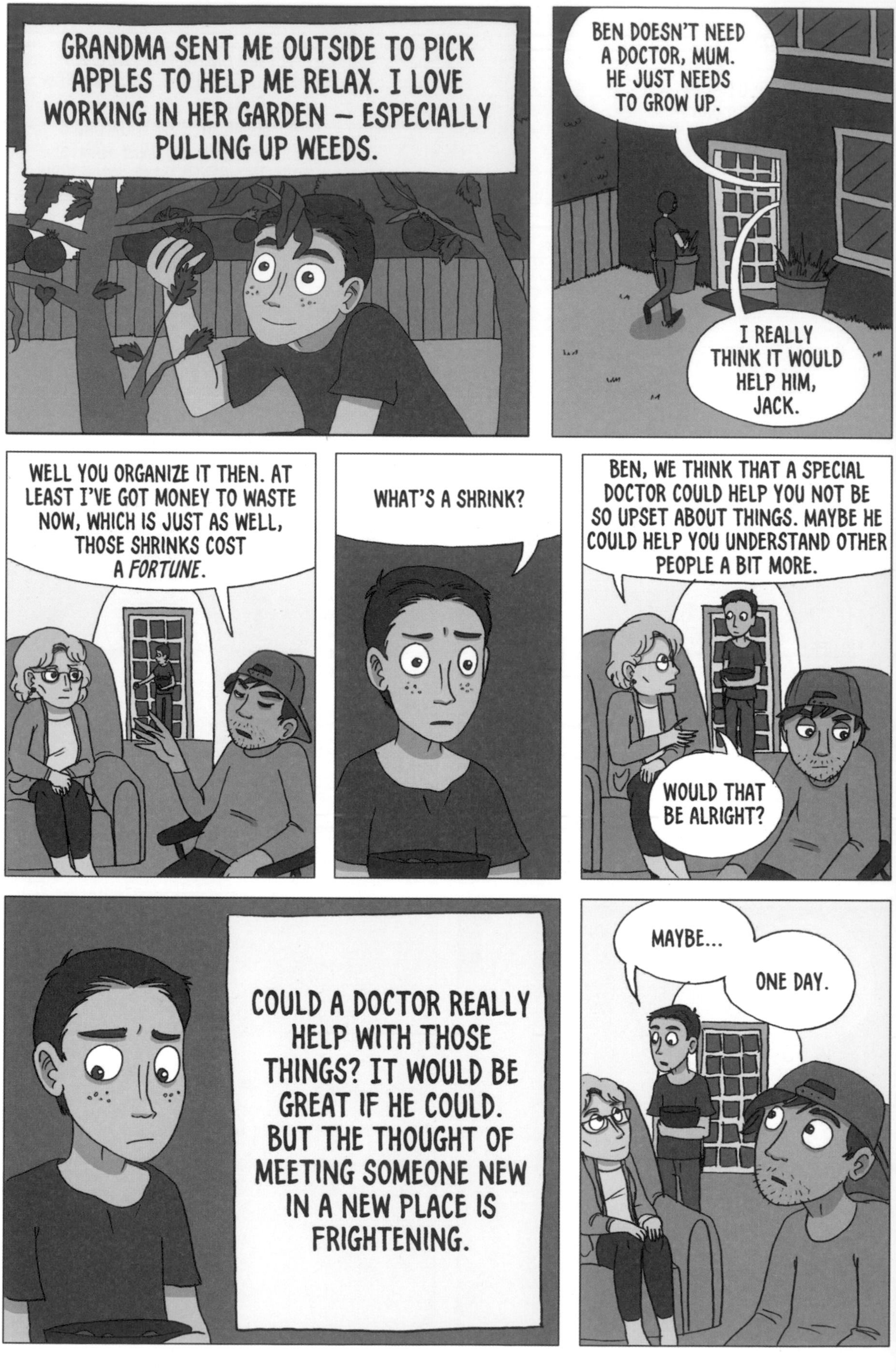
GRANDMA SENT ME OUTSIDE TO PICK APPLES TO HELP ME RELAX. I LOVE WORKING IN HER GARDEN – ESPECIALLY PULLING UP WEEDS.
BEN DOESN'T NEED A DOCTOR, MUM. HE JUST NEEDS TO GROW UP.
I REALLY THINK IT WOULD HELP HIM, JACK.
WELL YOU ORGANIZE IT THEN. AT LEAST I'VE GOT MONEY TO WASTE NOW, WHICH IS JUST AS WELL, THOSE SHRINKS COST A *FORTUNE*.
WHAT'S A SHRINK?
BEN, WE THINK THAT A SPECIAL DOCTOR COULD HELP YOU NOT BE SO UPSET ABOUT THINGS. MAYBE HE COULD HELP YOU UNDERSTAND OTHER PEOPLE A BIT MORE.
WOULD THAT BE ALRIGHT?
COULD A DOCTOR REALLY HELP WITH THOSE THINGS? IT WOULD BE GREAT IF HE COULD. BUT THE THOUGHT OF MEETING SOMEONE NEW IN A NEW PLACE IS FRIGHTENING.
MAYBE...
ONE DAY.

CHAPTER 6: GROWING UP

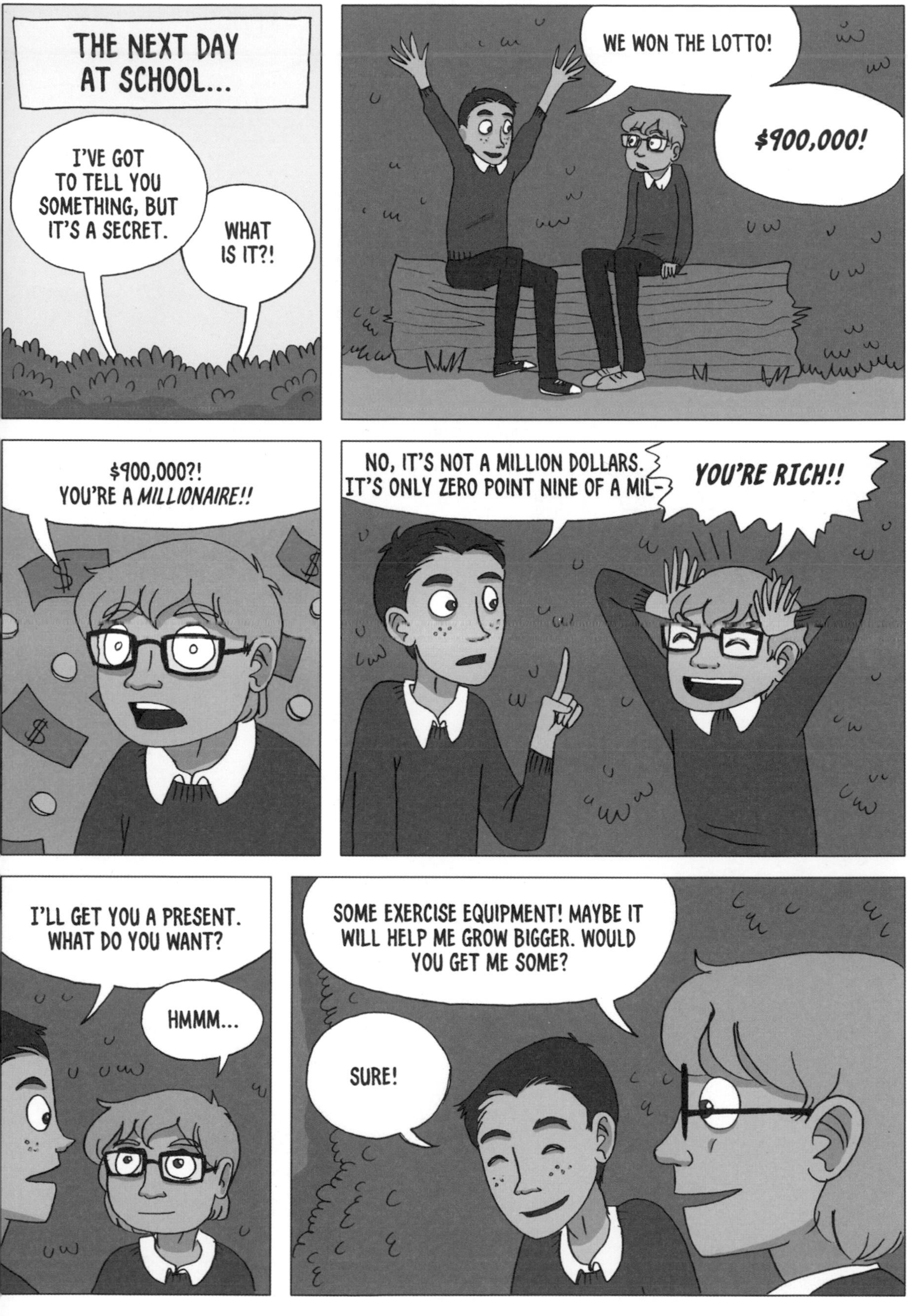
THE NEXT DAY AT SCHOOL...
I'VE GOT TO TELL YOU SOMETHING, BUT IT'S A SECRET.
WHAT IS IT?!
WE WON THE LOTTO!
$900,000!
$900,000?! YOU'RE A *MILLIONAIRE!!*
NO, IT'S NOT A MILLION DOLLARS. IT'S ONLY ZERO POINT NINE OF A MIL-
YOU'RE RICH!!
I'LL GET YOU A PRESENT. WHAT DO YOU WANT?
HMMM...
SOME EXERCISE EQUIPMENT! MAYBE IT WILL HELP ME GROW BIGGER. WOULD YOU GET ME SOME?
SURE!

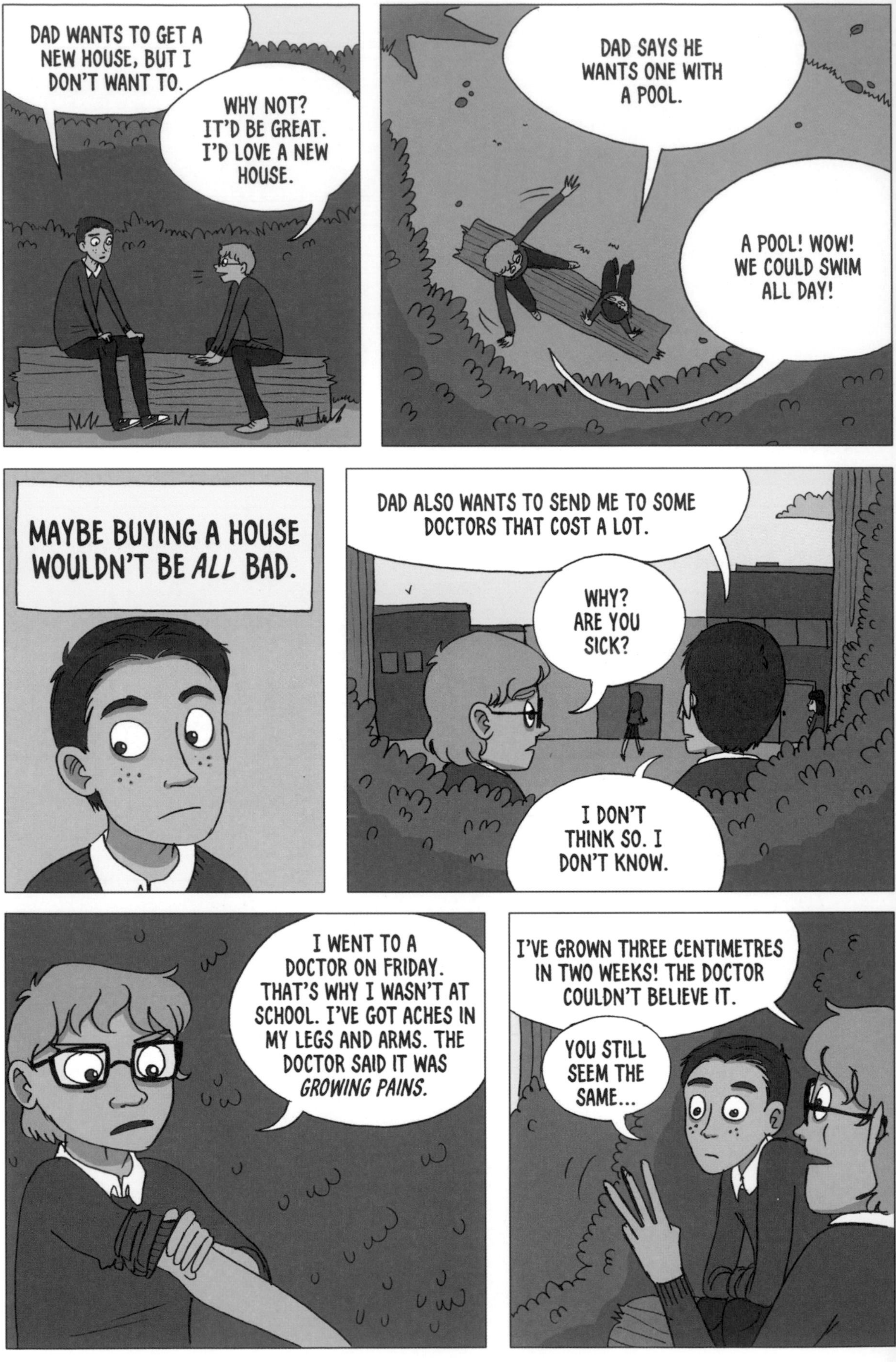
DAD WANTS TO GET A NEW HOUSE, BUT I DON'T WANT TO.
WHY NOT? IT'D BE GREAT. I'D LOVE A NEW HOUSE.
DAD SAYS HE WANTS ONE WITH A POOL.
A POOL! WOW! WE COULD SWIM ALL DAY!
MAYBE BUYING A HOUSE WOULDN'T BE *ALL* BAD.
DAD ALSO WANTS TO SEND ME TO SOME DOCTORS THAT COST A LOT.
WHY? ARE YOU SICK?
I DON'T THINK SO. I DON'T KNOW.
I WENT TO A DOCTOR ON FRIDAY. THAT'S WHY I WASN'T AT SCHOOL. I'VE GOT ACHES IN MY LEGS AND ARMS. THE DOCTOR SAID IT WAS *GROWING PAINS.*
I'VE GROWN THREE CENTIMETRES IN TWO WEEKS! THE DOCTOR COULDN'T BELIEVE IT.
YOU STILL SEEM THE SAME...

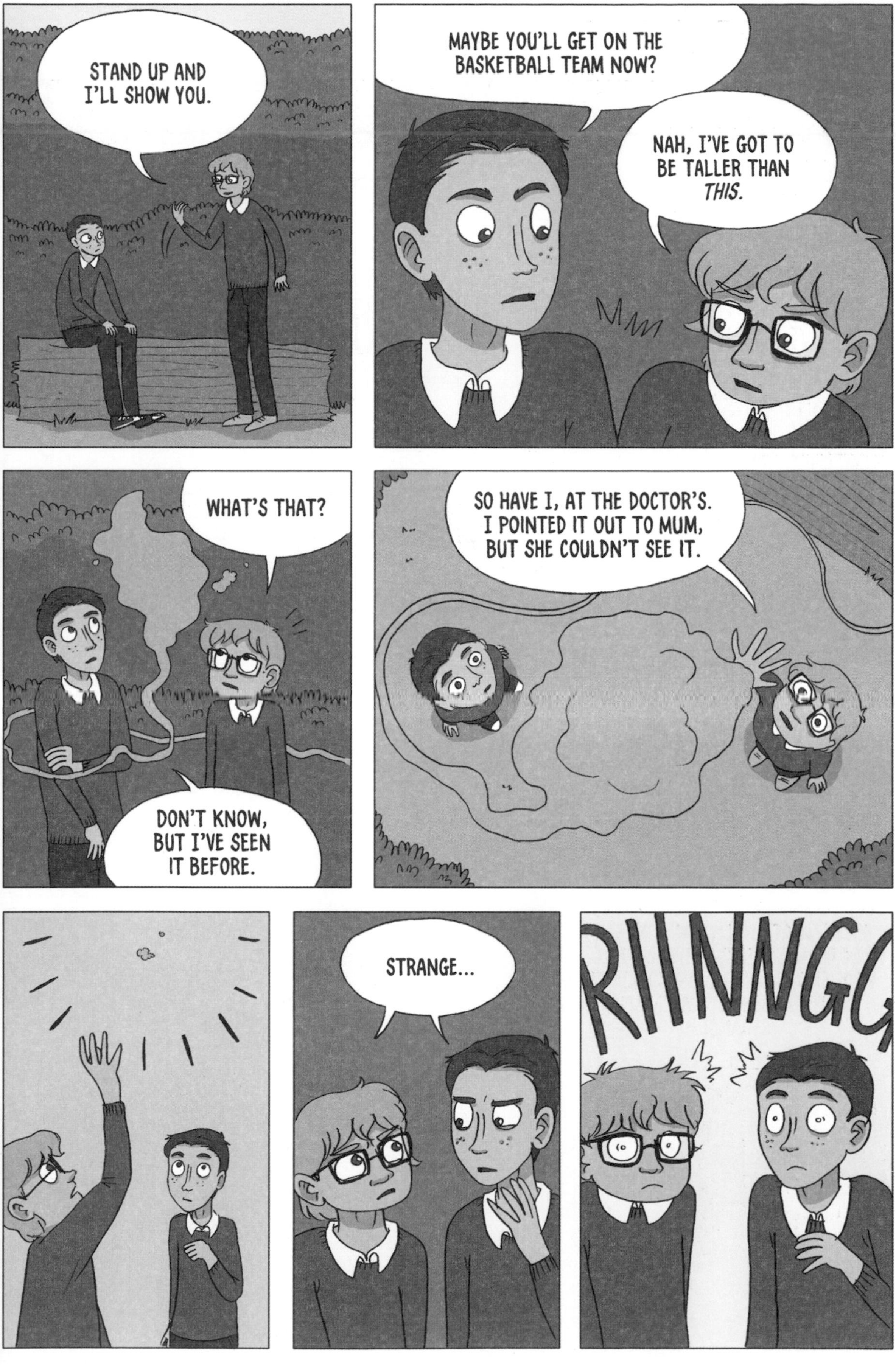

STAND UP AND I'LL SHOW YOU.
MAYBE YOU'LL GET ON THE BASKETBALL TEAM NOW?
NAH, I'VE GOT TO BE TALLER THAN *THIS.*
WHAT'S THAT?
DON'T KNOW, BUT I'VE SEEN IT BEFORE.
SO HAVE I, AT THE DOCTOR'S. I POINTED IT OUT TO MUM, BUT SHE COULDN'T SEE IT.
STRANGE...
RIINNG

CHAPTER 7: THE WISP

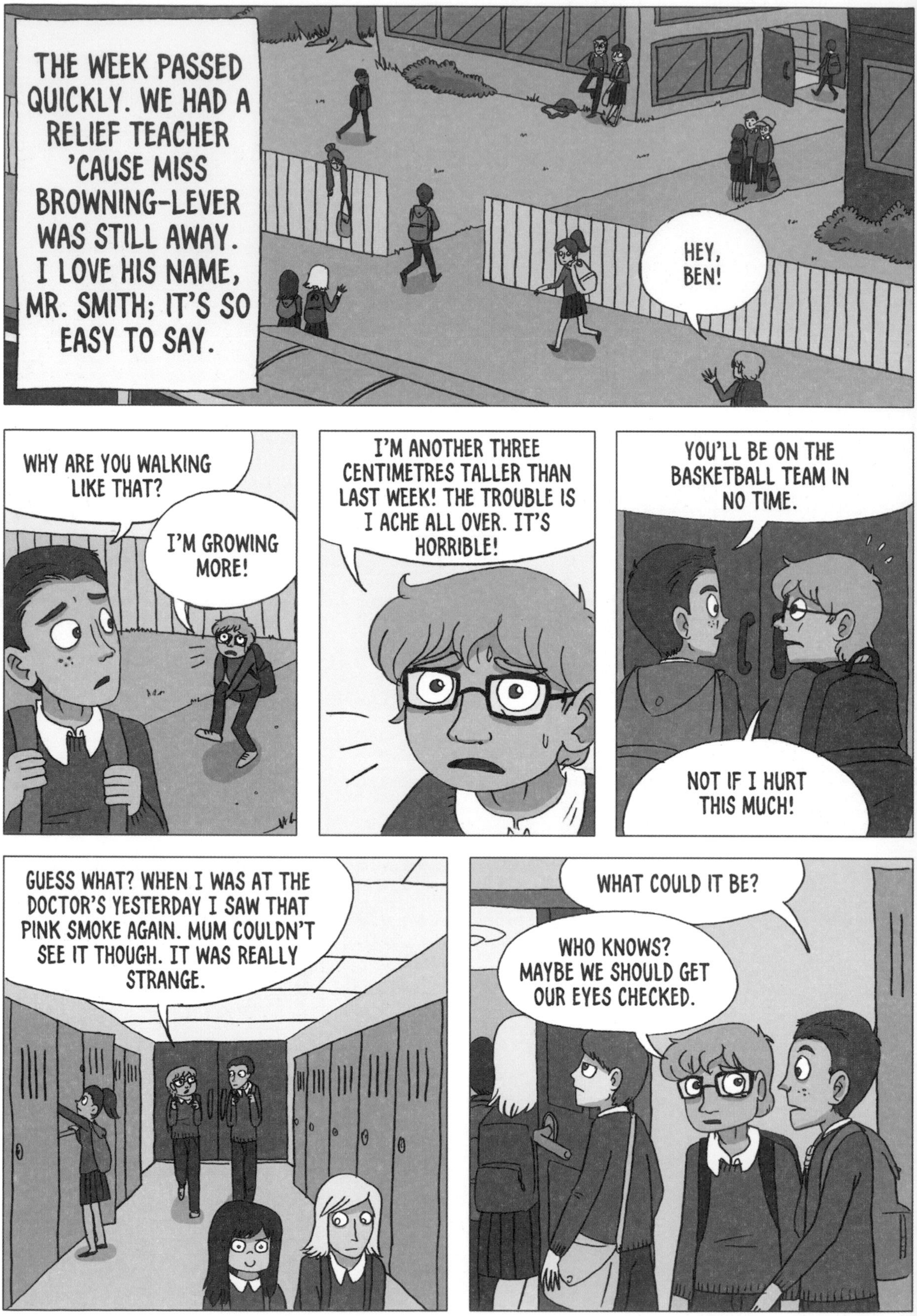
THE WEEK PASSED QUICKLY. WE HAD A RELIEF TEACHER 'CAUSE MISS BROWNING-LEVER WAS STILL AWAY. I LOVE HIS NAME, MR. SMITH; IT'S SO EASY TO SAY.
HEY, BEN!
WHY ARE YOU WALKING LIKE THAT?
I'M GROWING MORE!
I'M ANOTHER THREE CENTIMETRES TALLER THAN LAST WEEK! THE TROUBLE IS I ACHE ALL OVER. IT'S HORRIBLE!
YOU'LL BE ON THE BASKETBALL TEAM IN NO TIME.
NOT IF I HURT THIS MUCH!
GUESS WHAT? WHEN I WAS AT THE DOCTOR'S YESTERDAY I SAW THAT PINK SMOKE AGAIN. MUM COULDN'T SEE IT THOUGH. IT WAS REALLY STRANGE.
WHAT COULD IT BE?
WHO KNOWS? MAYBE WE SHOULD GET OUR EYES CHECKED.

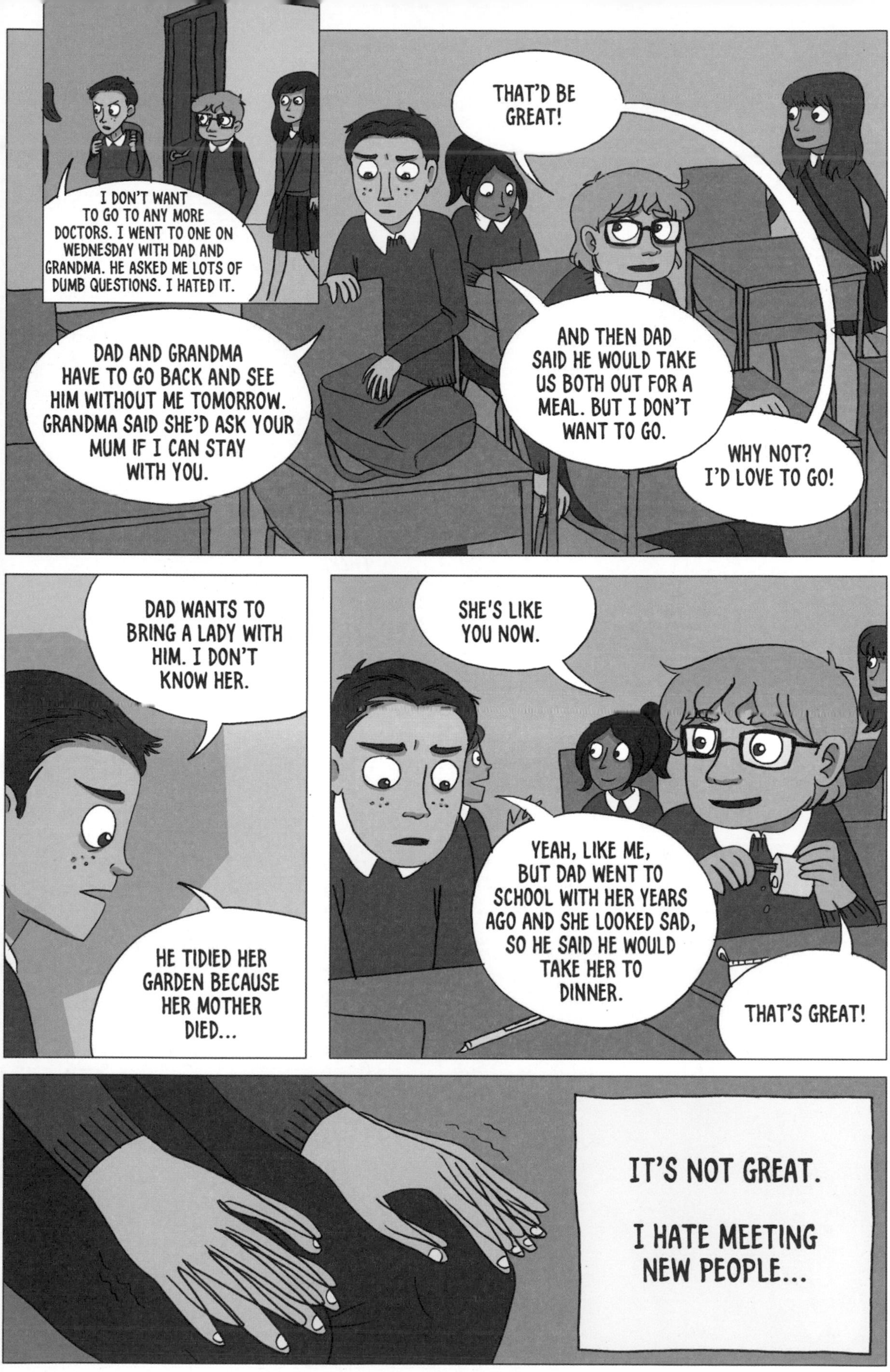
I DON'T WANT TO GO TO ANY MORE DOCTORS. I WENT TO ONE ON WEDNESDAY WITH DAD AND GRANDMA. HE ASKED ME LOTS OF DUMB QUESTIONS. I HATED IT.
DAD AND GRANDMA HAVE TO GO BACK AND SEE HIM WITHOUT ME TOMORROW. GRANDMA SAID SHE'D ASK YOUR MUM IF I CAN STAY WITH YOU.
THAT'D BE GREAT!
AND THEN DAD SAID HE WOULD TAKE US BOTH OUT FOR A MEAL. BUT I DON'T WANT TO GO.
WHY NOT? I'D LOVE TO GO!
DAD WANTS TO BRING A LADY WITH HIM. I DON'T KNOW HER.
HE TIDIED HER GARDEN BECAUSE HER MOTHER DIED...
SHE'S LIKE YOU NOW.
YEAH, LIKE ME, BUT DAD WENT TO SCHOOL WITH HER YEARS AGO AND SHE LOOKED SAD, SO HE SAID HE WOULD TAKE HER TO DINNER.
THAT'S GREAT!
IT'S NOT GREAT.
I HATE MEETING NEW PEOPLE...

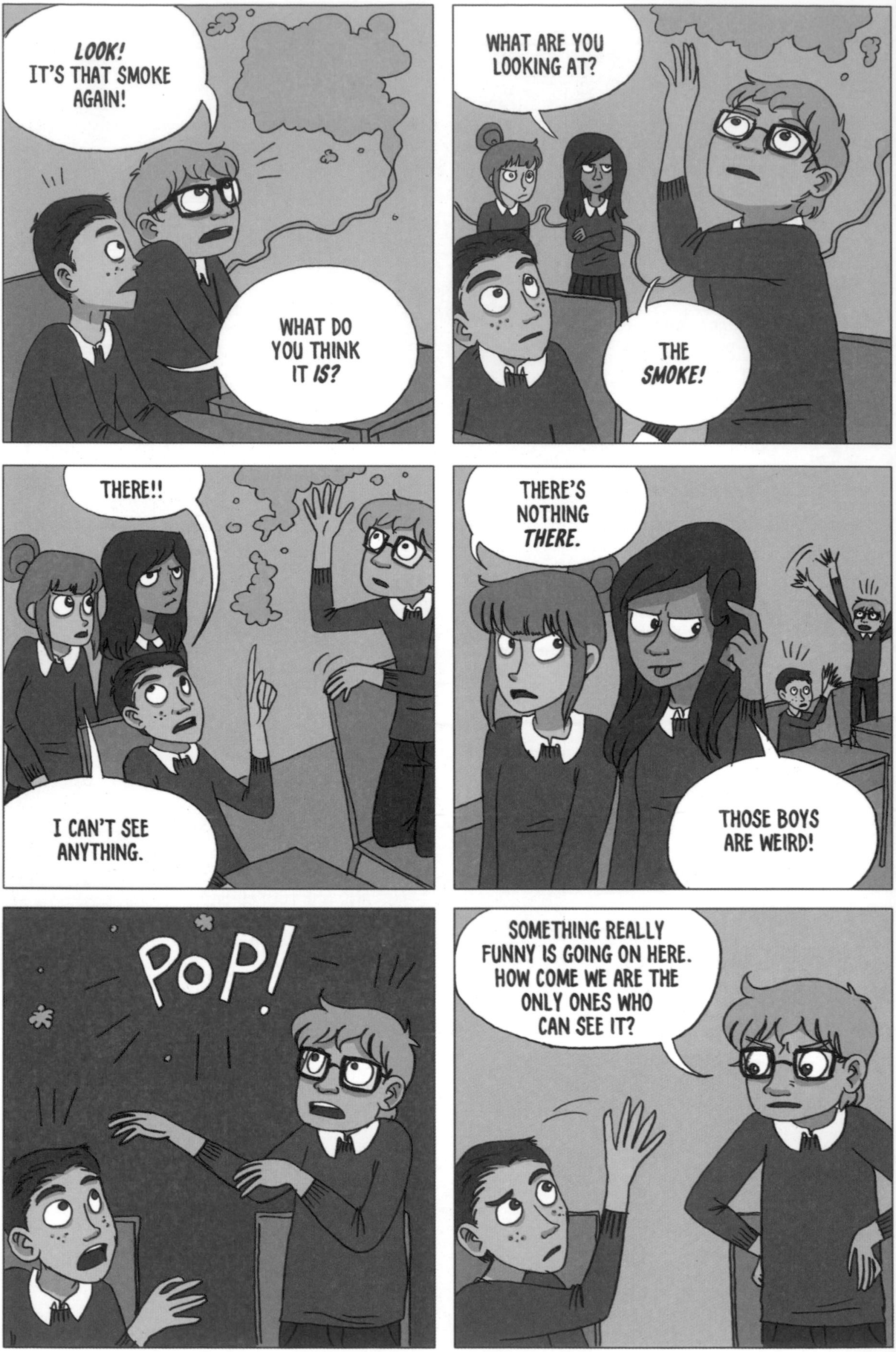
LOOK! IT'S THAT SMOKE AGAIN!
WHAT DO YOU THINK IT IS?
WHAT ARE YOU LOOKING AT?
THE SMOKE!
THERE!!
I CAN'T SEE ANYTHING.
THERE'S NOTHING THERE.
THOSE BOYS ARE WEIRD!
POP!
SOMETHING REALLY FUNNY IS GOING ON HERE. HOW COME WE ARE THE ONLY ONES WHO CAN SEE IT?

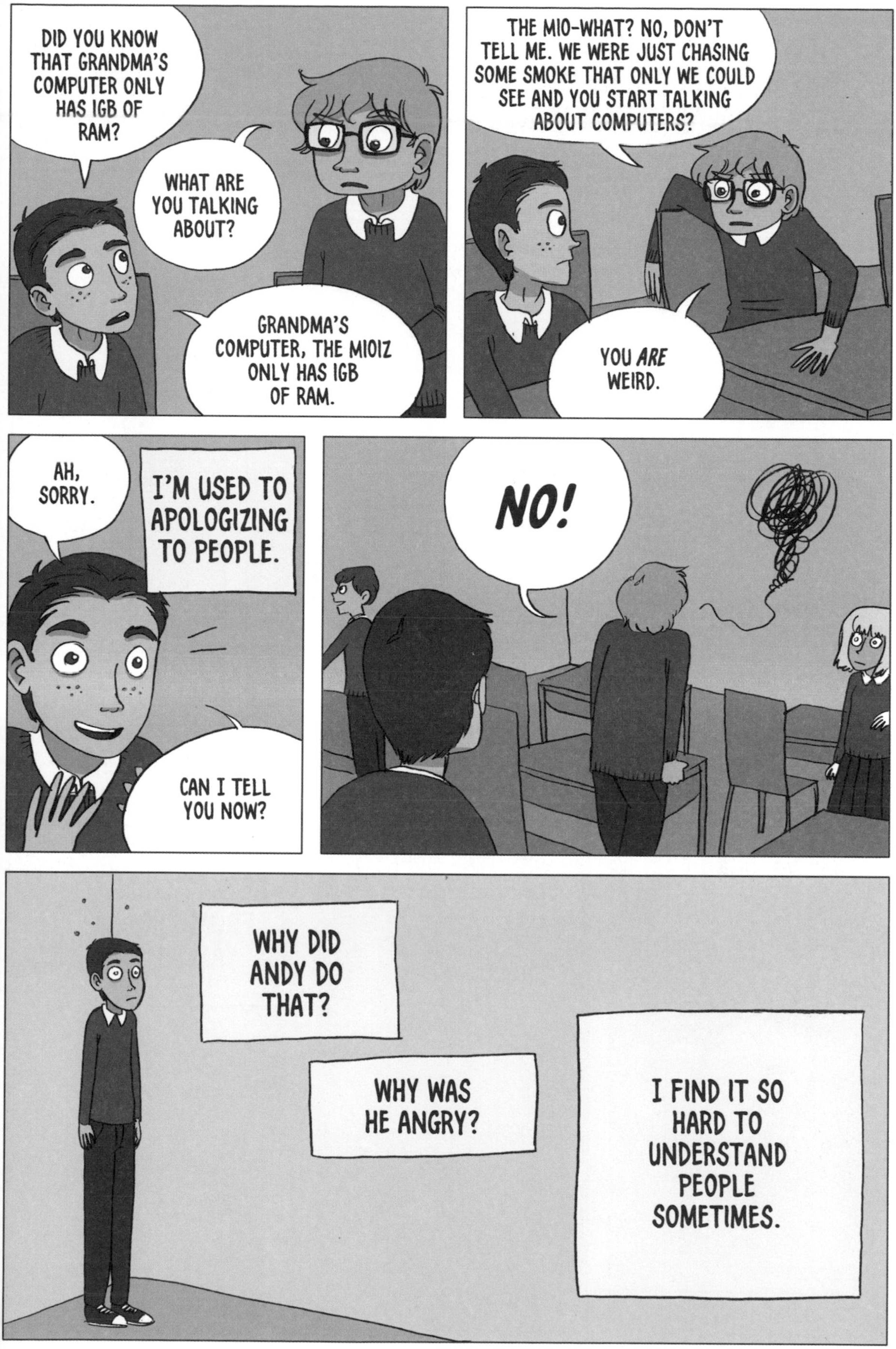
DID YOU KNOW THAT GRANDMA'S COMPUTER ONLY HAS 1GB OF RAM?
WHAT ARE YOU TALKING ABOUT?
GRANDMA'S COMPUTER, THE MIO12 ONLY HAS 1GB OF RAM.
THE MIO-WHAT? NO, DON'T TELL ME. WE WERE JUST CHASING SOME SMOKE THAT ONLY WE COULD SEE AND YOU START TALKING ABOUT COMPUTERS?
YOU *ARE* WEIRD.
AH, SORRY.
I'M USED TO APOLOGIZING TO PEOPLE.
CAN I TELL YOU NOW?
NO!
WHY DID ANDY DO THAT?
WHY WAS HE ANGRY?
I FIND IT SO HARD TO UNDERSTAND PEOPLE SOMETIMES.

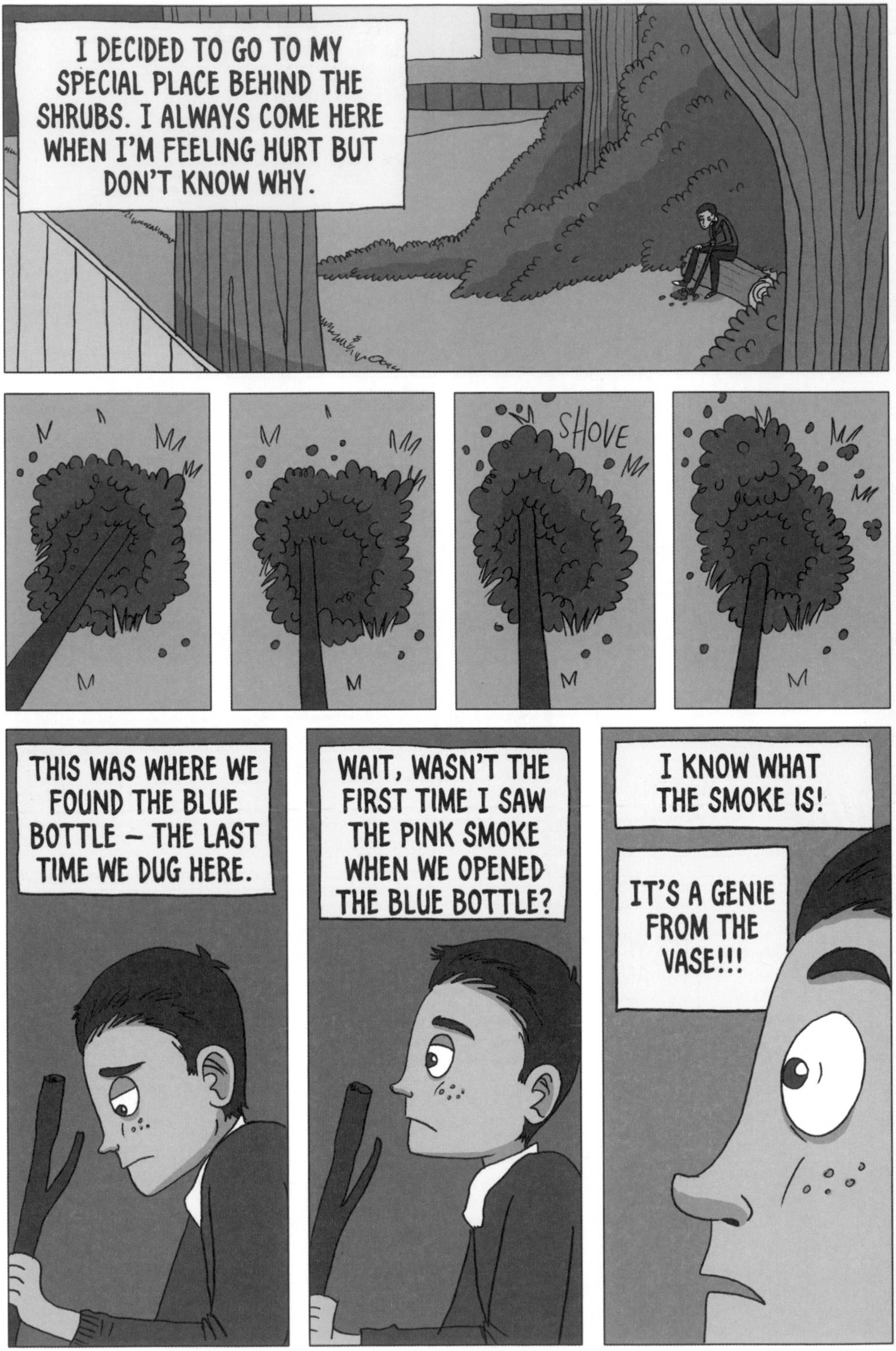
I DECIDED TO GO TO MY SPECIAL PLACE BEHIND THE SHRUBS. I ALWAYS COME HERE WHEN I'M FEELING HURT BUT DON'T KNOW WHY.
SHOVE
THIS WAS WHERE WE FOUND THE BLUE BOTTLE – THE LAST TIME WE DUG HERE.
WAIT, WASN'T THE FIRST TIME I SAW THE PINK SMOKE WHEN WE OPENED THE BLUE BOTTLE?
I KNOW WHAT THE SMOKE IS!
IT'S A GENIE FROM THE VASE!!!

CHAPTER 8: WHICH WISHES?

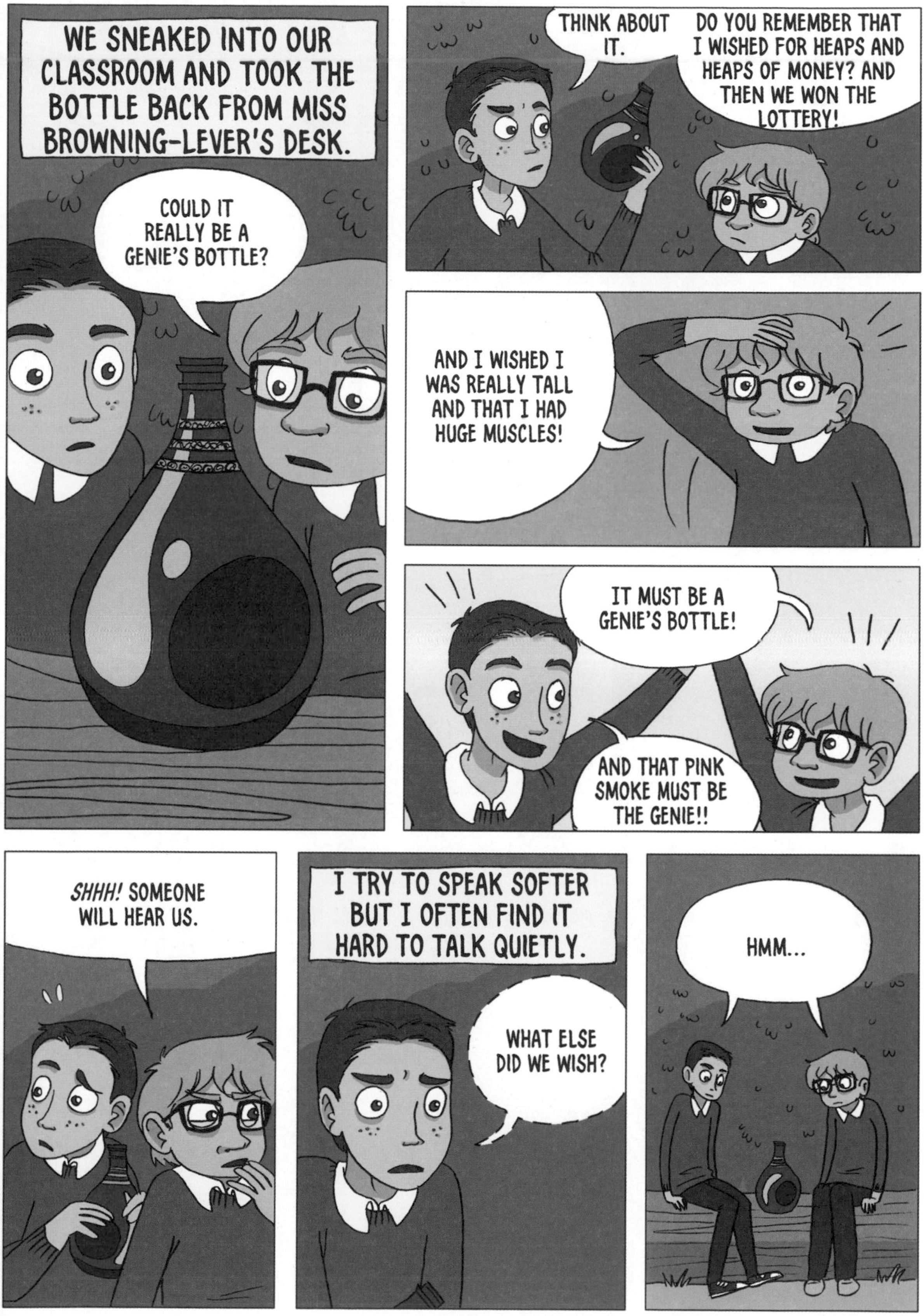
WE SNEAKED INTO OUR CLASSROOM AND TOOK THE BOTTLE BACK FROM MISS BROWNING-LEVER'S DESK.
COULD IT REALLY BE A GENIE'S BOTTLE?
THINK ABOUT IT.
DO YOU REMEMBER THAT I WISHED FOR HEAPS AND HEAPS OF MONEY? AND THEN WE WON THE LOTTERY!
AND I WISHED I WAS REALLY TALL AND THAT I HAD HUGE MUSCLES!
IT MUST BE A GENIE'S BOTTLE!
AND THAT PINK SMOKE MUST BE THE GENIE!!
SHHH! SOMEONE WILL HEAR US.
I TRY TO SPEAK SOFTER BUT I OFTEN FIND IT HARD TO TALK QUIETLY.
WHAT ELSE DID WE WISH?
HMM...

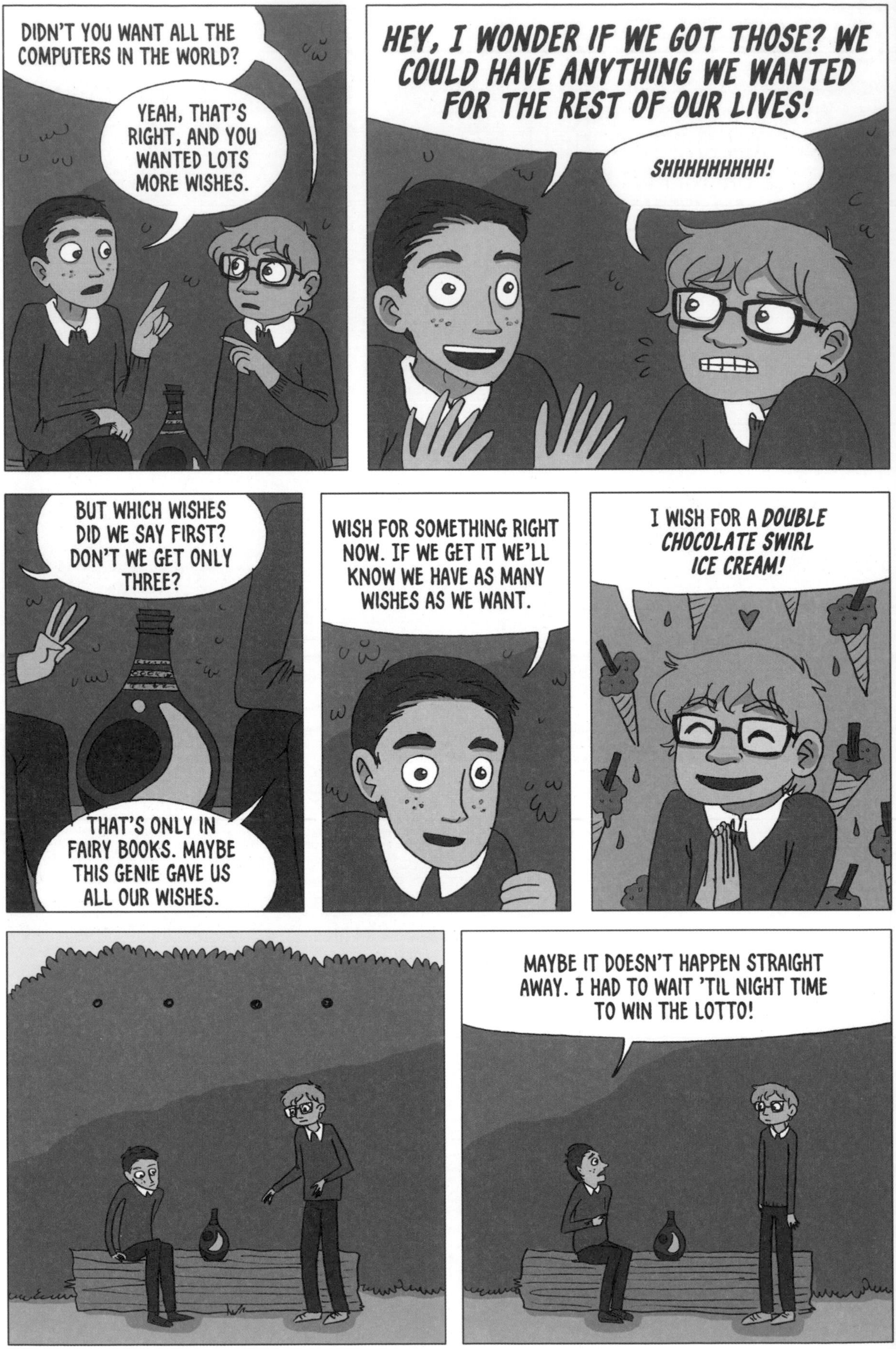
DIDN'T YOU WANT ALL THE COMPUTERS IN THE WORLD?
YEAH, THAT'S RIGHT, AND YOU WANTED LOTS MORE WISHES.
HEY, I WONDER IF WE GOT THOSE? WE COULD HAVE ANYTHING WE WANTED FOR THE REST OF OUR LIVES!
SHHHHHHHHH!
BUT WHICH WISHES DID WE SAY FIRST? DON'T WE GET ONLY THREE?
THAT'S ONLY IN FAIRY BOOKS. MAYBE THIS GENIE GAVE US ALL OUR WISHES.
WISH FOR SOMETHING RIGHT NOW. IF WE GET IT WE'LL KNOW WE HAVE AS MANY WISHES AS WE WANT.
I WISH FOR A *DOUBLE CHOCOLATE SWIRL ICE CREAM!*
MAYBE IT DOESN'T HAPPEN STRAIGHT AWAY. I HAD TO WAIT 'TIL NIGHT TIME TO WIN THE LOTTO!

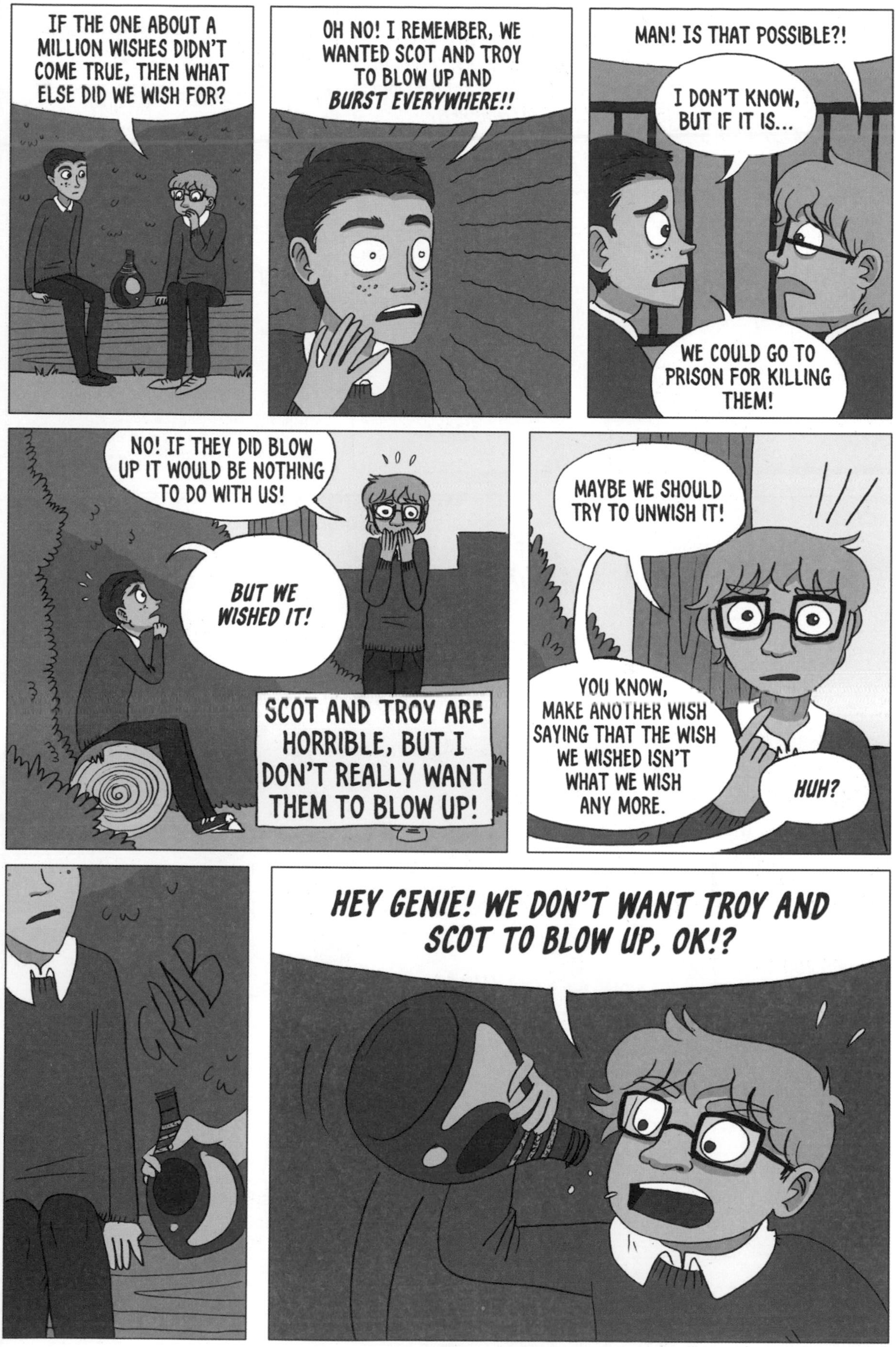
IF THE ONE ABOUT A MILLION WISHES DIDN'T COME TRUE, THEN WHAT ELSE DID WE WISH FOR?
OH NO! I REMEMBER, WE WANTED SCOT AND TROY TO BLOW UP AND *BURST EVERYWHERE!!*
MAN! IS THAT POSSIBLE?!
I DON'T KNOW, BUT IF IT IS...
WE COULD GO TO PRISON FOR KILLING THEM!
NO! IF THEY DID BLOW UP IT WOULD BE NOTHING TO DO WITH US!
BUT WE WISHED IT!
SCOT AND TROY ARE HORRIBLE, BUT I DON'T REALLY WANT THEM TO BLOW UP!
MAYBE WE SHOULD TRY TO UNWISH IT!
YOU KNOW, MAKE ANOTHER WISH SAYING THAT THE WISH WE WISHED ISN'T WHAT WE WISH ANY MORE.
HUH?
GRAB
HEY GENIE! WE DON'T WANT TROY AND SCOT TO BLOW UP, OK!?

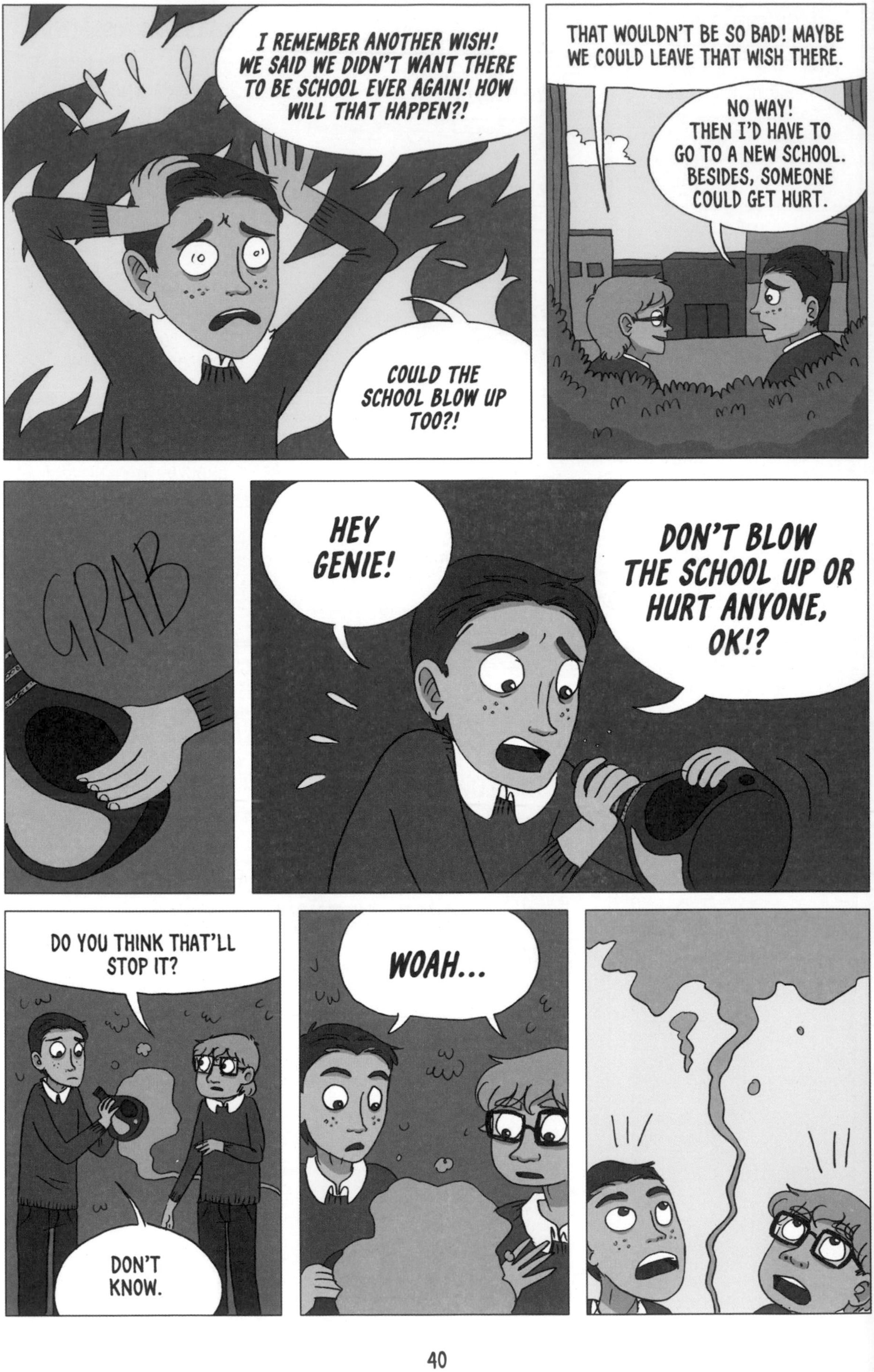
I REMEMBER ANOTHER WISH! WE SAID WE DIDN'T WANT THERE TO BE SCHOOL EVER AGAIN! HOW WILL THAT HAPPEN?!
COULD THE SCHOOL BLOW UP TOO?!
THAT WOULDN'T BE SO BAD! MAYBE WE COULD LEAVE THAT WISH THERE.
NO WAY! THEN I'D HAVE TO GO TO A NEW SCHOOL. BESIDES, SOMEONE COULD GET HURT.
GRAB
HEY GENIE!
DON'T BLOW THE SCHOOL UP OR HURT ANYONE, OK!?
DO YOU THINK THAT'LL STOP IT?
DON'T KNOW.
WOAH...

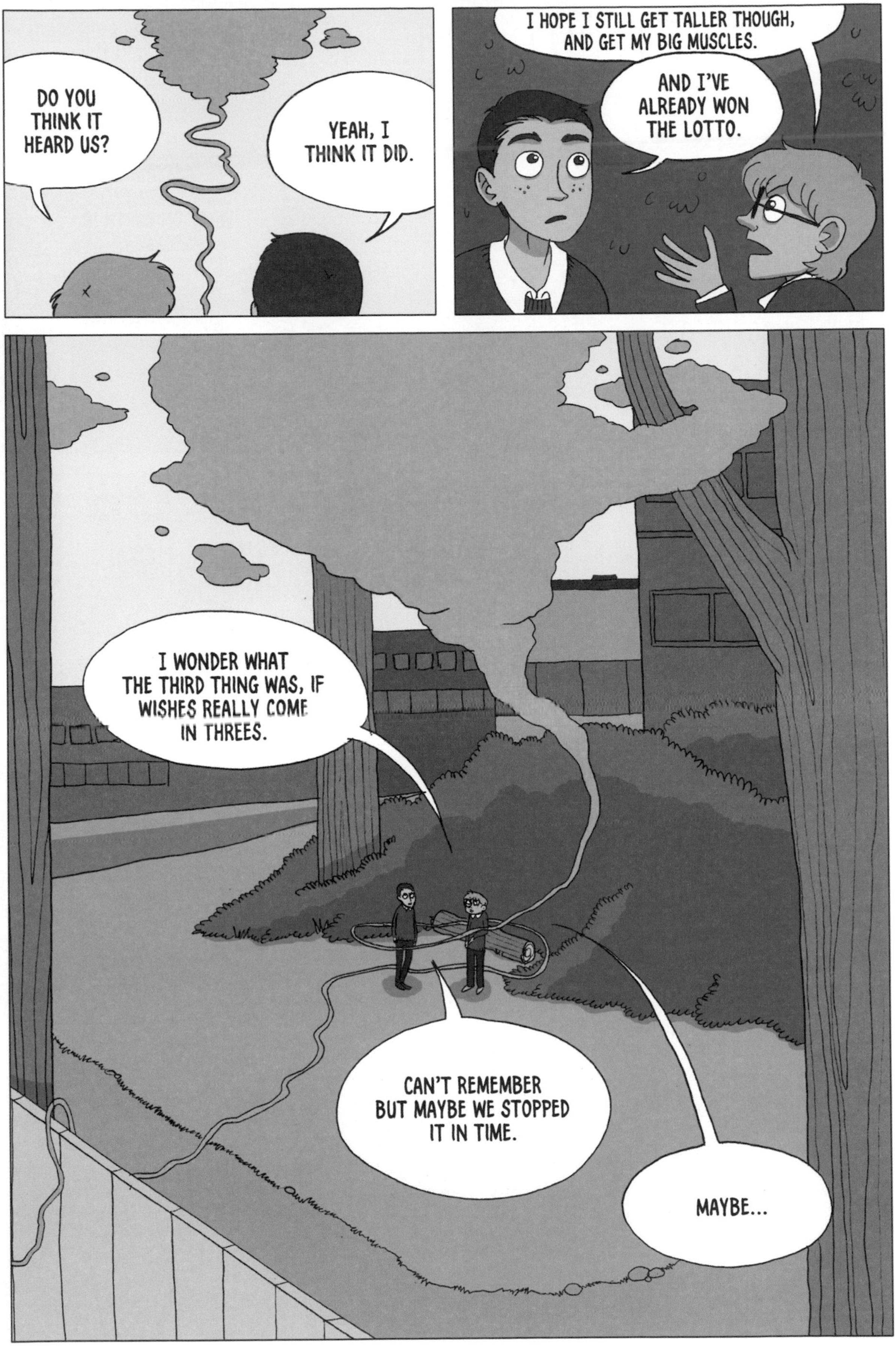
DO YOU THINK IT HEARD US?
YEAH, I THINK IT DID.
I HOPE I STILL GET TALLER THOUGH, AND GET MY BIG MUSCLES.
AND I'VE ALREADY WON THE LOTTO.
I WONDER WHAT THE THIRD THING WAS, IF WISHES REALLY COME IN THREES.
CAN'T REMEMBER BUT MAYBE WE STOPPED IT IN TIME.
MAYBE...

CHAPTER 9: ASPERGER SYNDROME

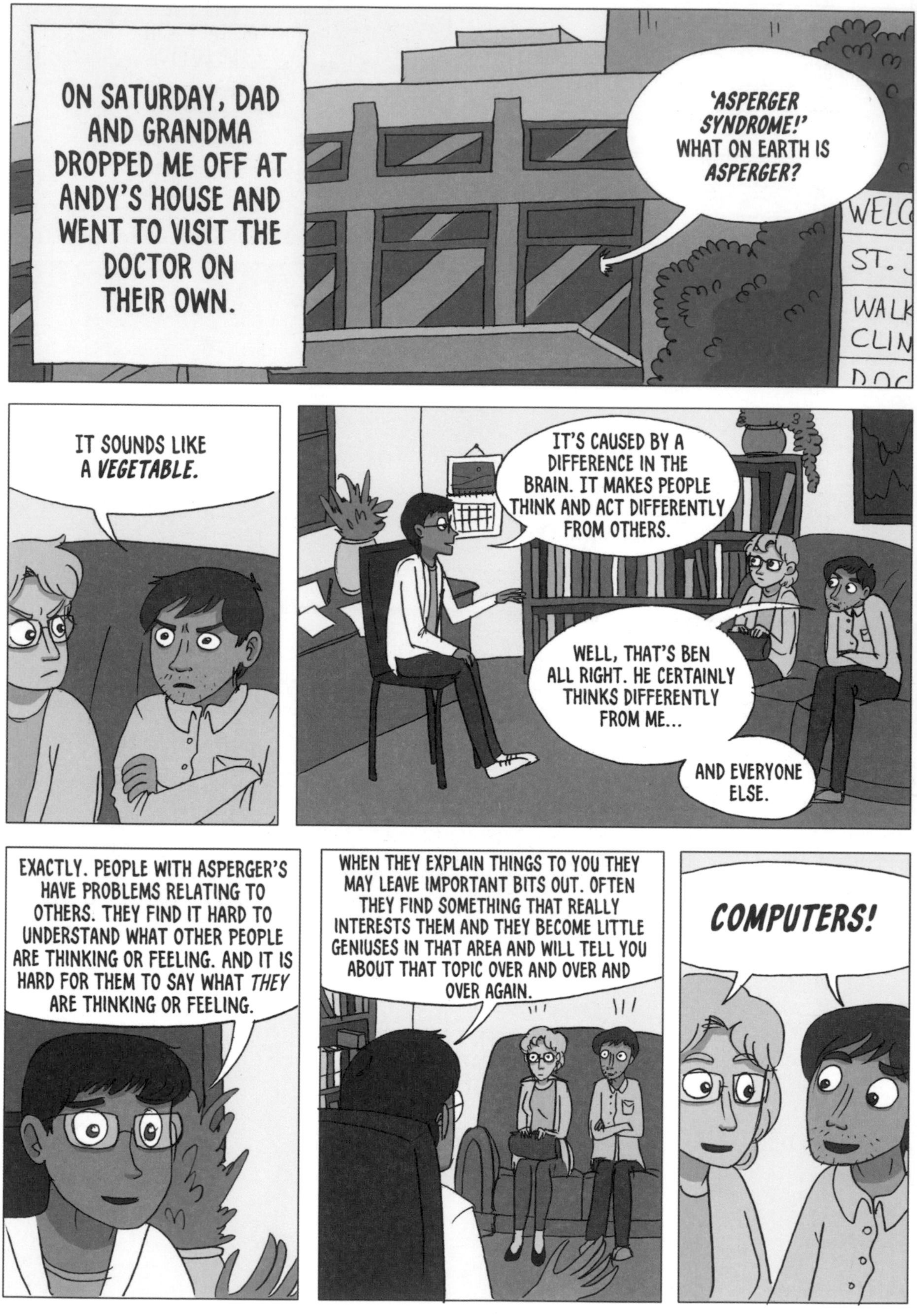
ON SATURDAY, DAD AND GRANDMA DROPPED ME OFF AT ANDY'S HOUSE AND WENT TO VISIT THE DOCTOR ON THEIR OWN.
'ASPERGER SYNDROME!' WHAT ON EARTH IS ASPERGER?
IT SOUNDS LIKE A VEGETABLE.
IT'S CAUSED BY A DIFFERENCE IN THE BRAIN. IT MAKES PEOPLE THINK AND ACT DIFFERENTLY FROM OTHERS.
WELL, THAT'S BEN ALL RIGHT. HE CERTAINLY THINKS DIFFERENTLY FROM ME...
AND EVERYONE ELSE.
EXACTLY. PEOPLE WITH ASPERGER'S HAVE PROBLEMS RELATING TO OTHERS. THEY FIND IT HARD TO UNDERSTAND WHAT OTHER PEOPLE ARE THINKING OR FEELING. AND IT IS HARD FOR THEM TO SAY WHAT THEY ARE THINKING OR FEELING.
WHEN THEY EXPLAIN THINGS TO YOU THEY MAY LEAVE IMPORTANT BITS OUT. OFTEN THEY FIND SOMETHING THAT REALLY INTERESTS THEM AND THEY BECOME LITTLE GENIUSES IN THAT AREA AND WILL TELL YOU ABOUT THAT TOPIC OVER AND OVER AND OVER AGAIN.
COMPUTERS!

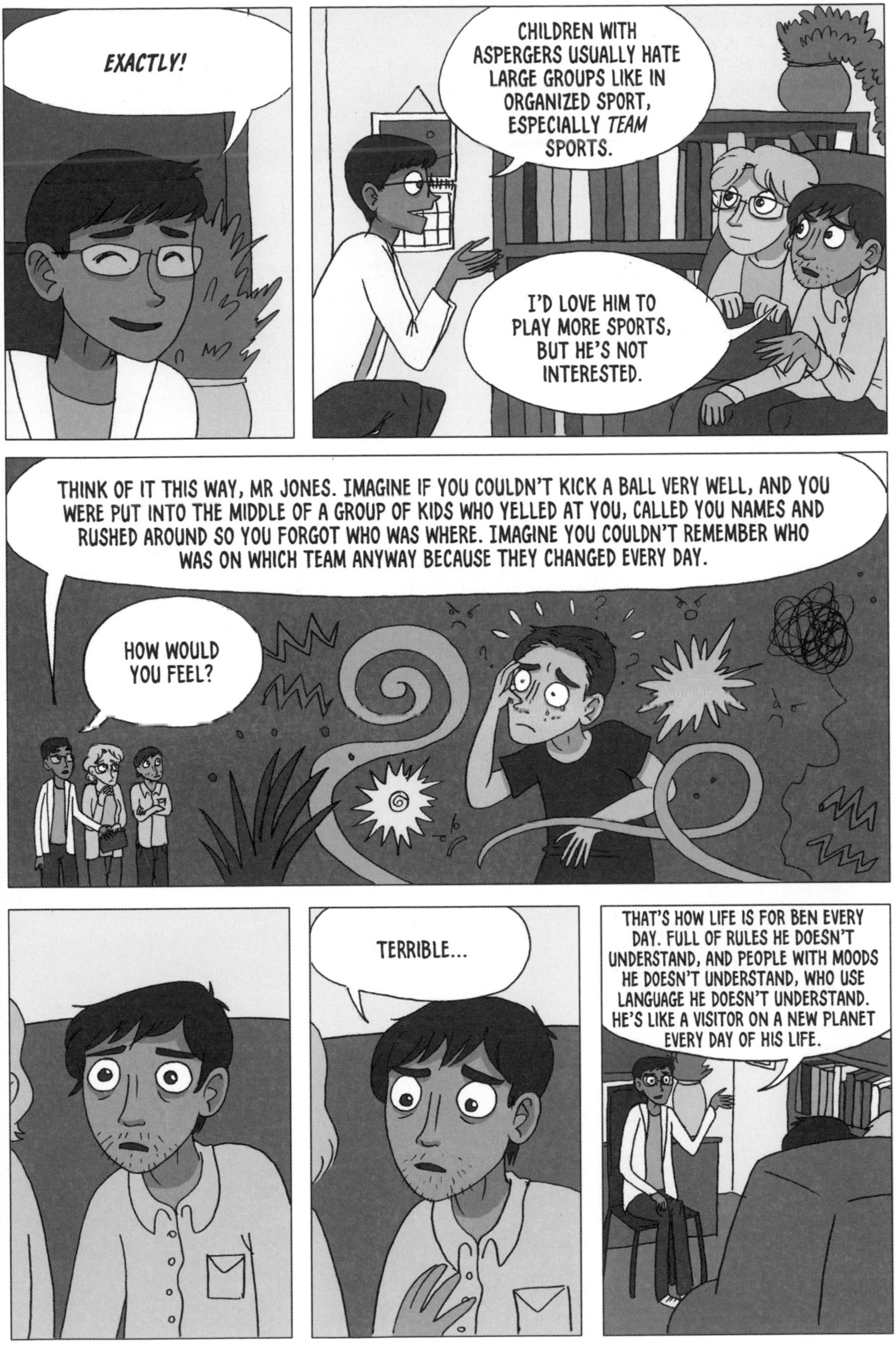
EXACTLY!
CHILDREN WITH ASPERGERS USUALLY HATE LARGE GROUPS LIKE IN ORGANIZED SPORT, ESPECIALLY *TEAM* SPORTS.
I'D LOVE HIM TO PLAY MORE SPORTS, BUT HE'S NOT INTERESTED.
THINK OF IT THIS WAY, MR JONES. IMAGINE IF YOU COULDN'T KICK A BALL VERY WELL, AND YOU WERE PUT INTO THE MIDDLE OF A GROUP OF KIDS WHO YELLED AT YOU, CALLED YOU NAMES AND RUSHED AROUND SO YOU FORGOT WHO WAS WHERE. IMAGINE YOU COULDN'T REMEMBER WHO WAS ON WHICH TEAM ANYWAY BECAUSE THEY CHANGED EVERY DAY.
HOW WOULD YOU FEEL?
TERRIBLE...
THAT'S HOW LIFE IS FOR BEN EVERY DAY. FULL OF RULES HE DOESN'T UNDERSTAND, AND PEOPLE WITH MOODS HE DOESN'T UNDERSTAND, WHO USE LANGUAGE HE DOESN'T UNDERSTAND. HE'S LIKE A VISITOR ON A NEW PLANET EVERY DAY OF HIS LIFE.

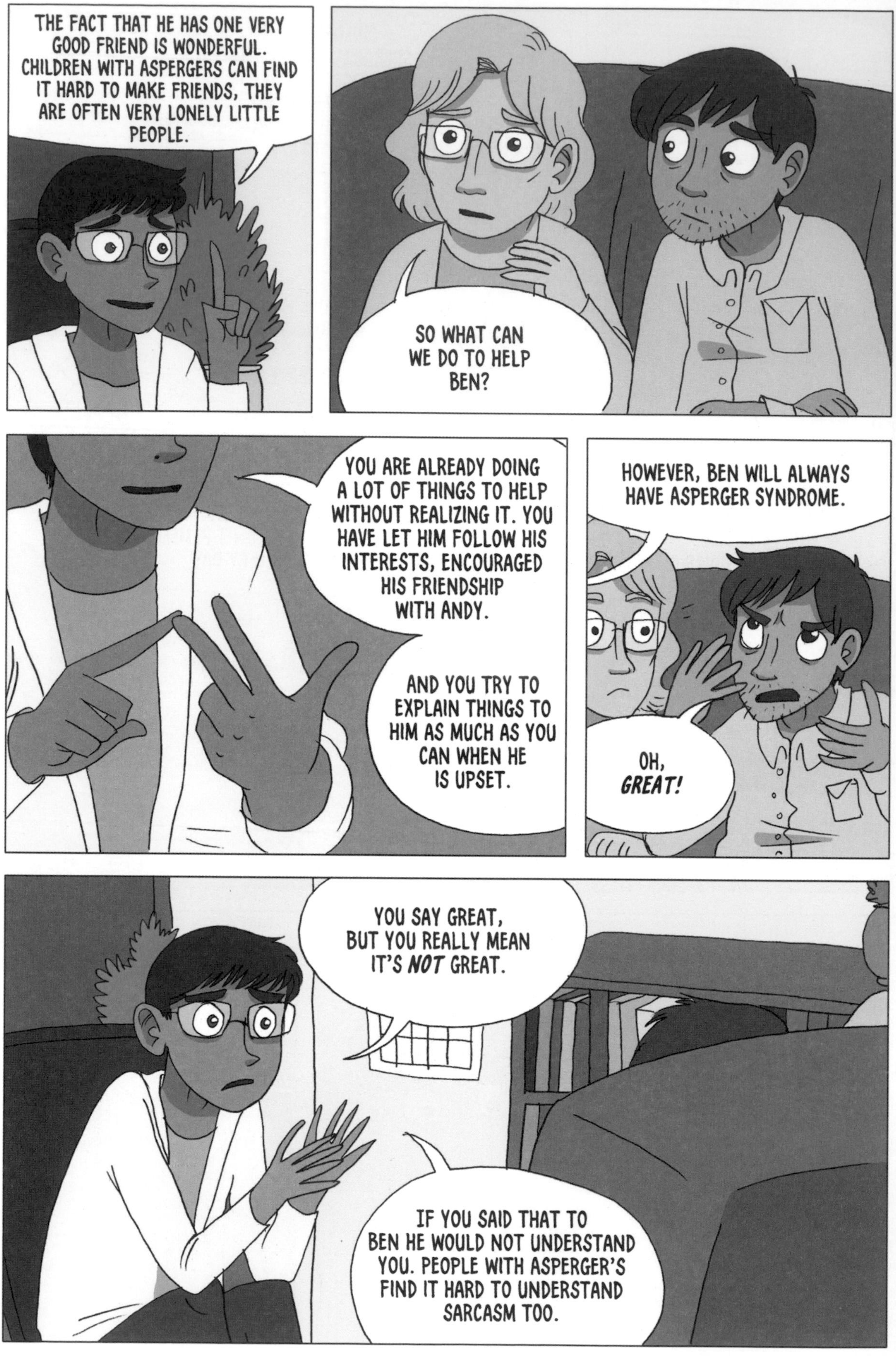
THE FACT THAT HE HAS ONE VERY GOOD FRIEND IS WONDERFUL. CHILDREN WITH ASPERGERS CAN FIND IT HARD TO MAKE FRIENDS, THEY ARE OFTEN VERY LONELY LITTLE PEOPLE.
SO WHAT CAN WE DO TO HELP BEN?
YOU ARE ALREADY DOING A LOT OF THINGS TO HELP WITHOUT REALIZING IT. YOU HAVE LET HIM FOLLOW HIS INTERESTS, ENCOURAGED HIS FRIENDSHIP WITH ANDY.
AND YOU TRY TO EXPLAIN THINGS TO HIM AS MUCH AS YOU CAN WHEN HE IS UPSET.
HOWEVER, BEN WILL ALWAYS HAVE ASPERGER SYNDROME.
OH, *GREAT!*
YOU SAY GREAT, BUT YOU REALLY MEAN IT'S *NOT* GREAT.
IF YOU SAID THAT TO BEN HE WOULD NOT UNDERSTAND YOU. PEOPLE WITH ASPERGER'S FIND IT HARD TO UNDERSTAND SARCASM TOO.

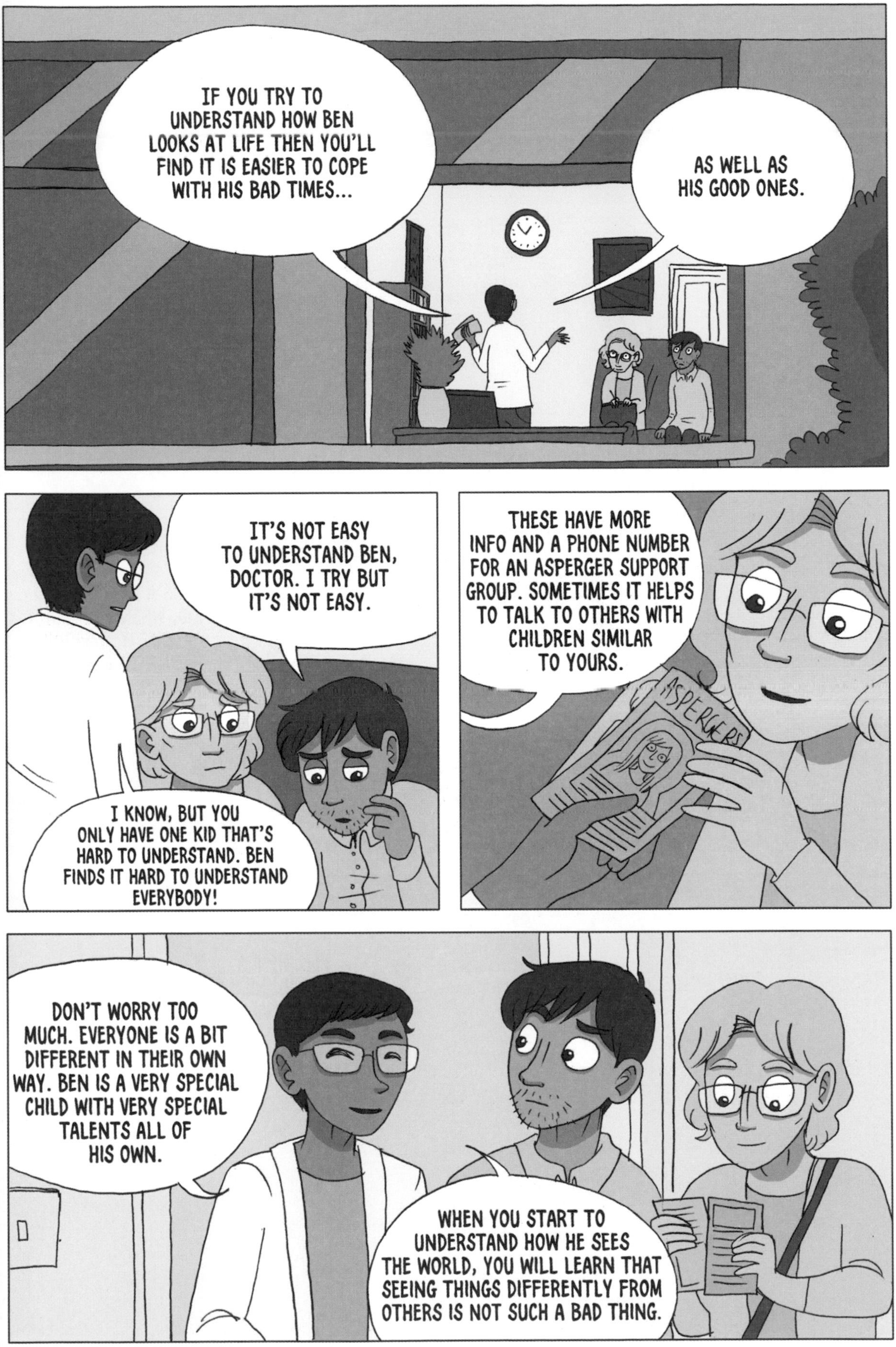
IF YOU TRY TO UNDERSTAND HOW BEN LOOKS AT LIFE THEN YOU'LL FIND IT IS EASIER TO COPE WITH HIS BAD TIMES...
AS WELL AS HIS GOOD ONES.
IT'S NOT EASY TO UNDERSTAND BEN, DOCTOR. I TRY BUT IT'S NOT EASY.
I KNOW, BUT YOU ONLY HAVE ONE KID THAT'S HARD TO UNDERSTAND. BEN FINDS IT HARD TO UNDERSTAND EVERYBODY!
THESE HAVE MORE INFO AND A PHONE NUMBER FOR AN ASPERGER SUPPORT GROUP. SOMETIMES IT HELPS TO TALK TO OTHERS WITH CHILDREN SIMILAR TO YOURS.
ASPERGERS
DON'T WORRY TOO MUCH. EVERYONE IS A BIT DIFFERENT IN THEIR OWN WAY. BEN IS A VERY SPECIAL CHILD WITH VERY SPECIAL TALENTS ALL OF HIS OWN.
WHEN YOU START TO UNDERSTAND HOW HE SEES THE WORLD, YOU WILL LEARN THAT SEEING THINGS DIFFERENTLY FROM OTHERS IS NOT SUCH A BAD THING.

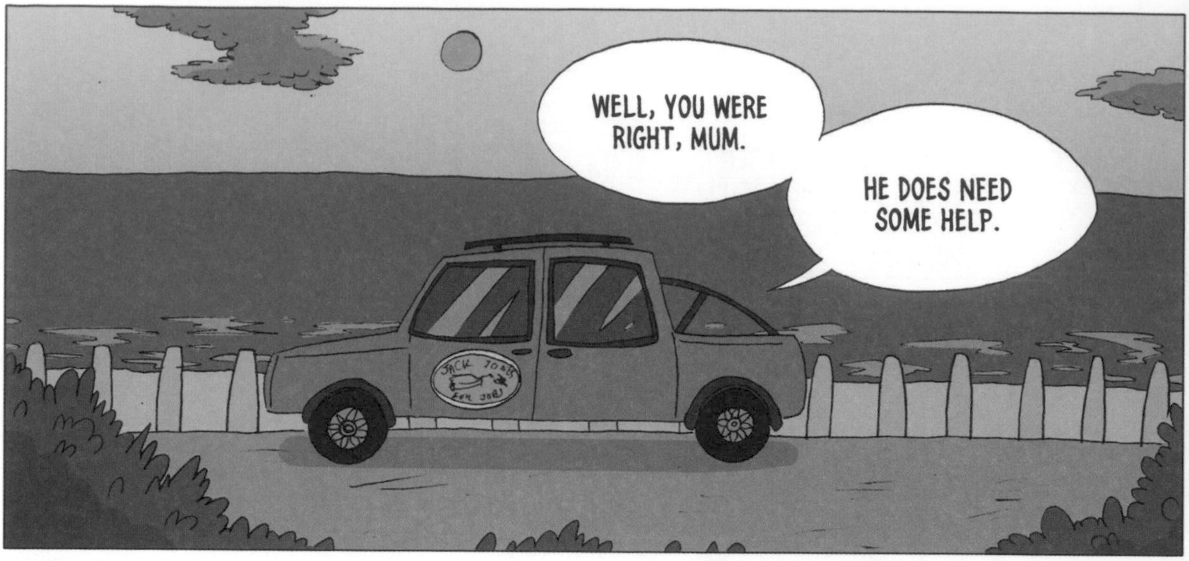
WELL, YOU WERE RIGHT, MUM.
HE DOES NEED SOME HELP.

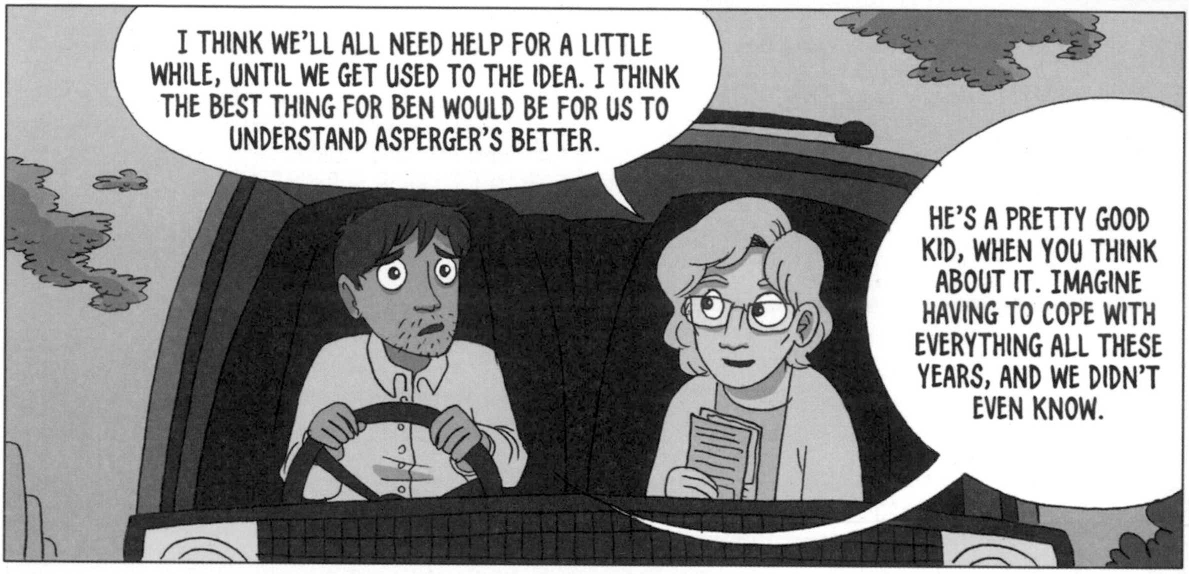
I THINK WE'LL ALL NEED HELP FOR A LITTLE WHILE, UNTIL WE GET USED TO THE IDEA. I THINK THE BEST THING FOR BEN WOULD BE FOR US TO UNDERSTAND ASPERGER'S BETTER.
HE'S A PRETTY GOOD KID, WHEN YOU THINK ABOUT IT. IMAGINE HAVING TO COPE WITH EVERYTHING ALL THESE YEARS, AND WE DIDN'T EVEN KNOW.

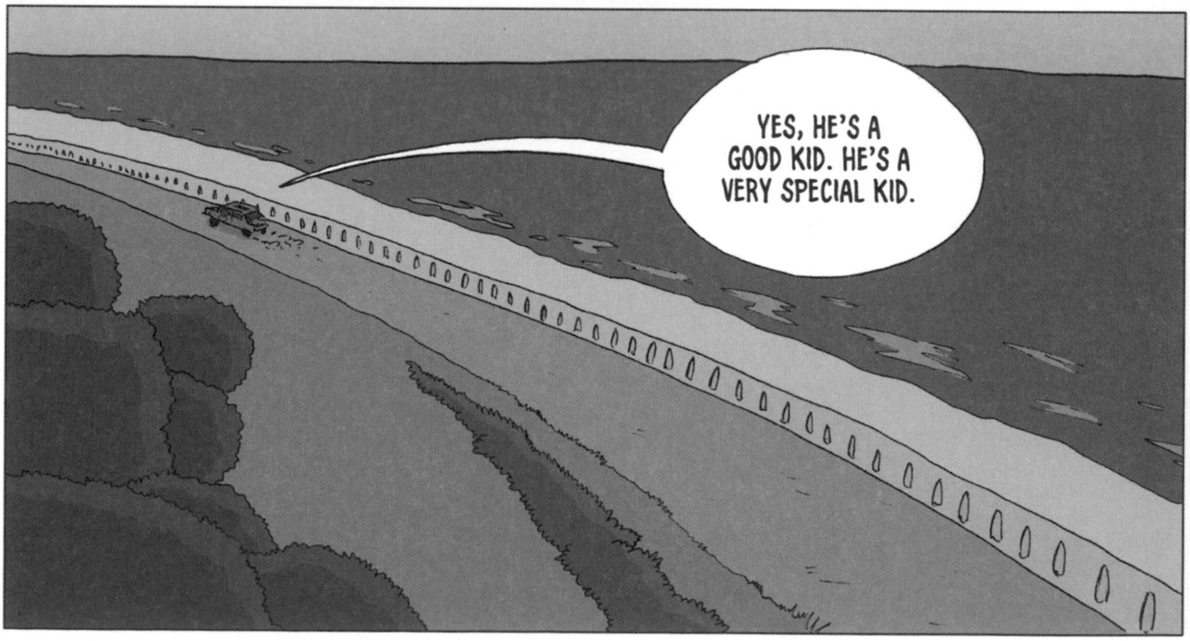
YES, HE'S A GOOD KID. HE'S A VERY SPECIAL KID.

CHAPTER 10: SUE

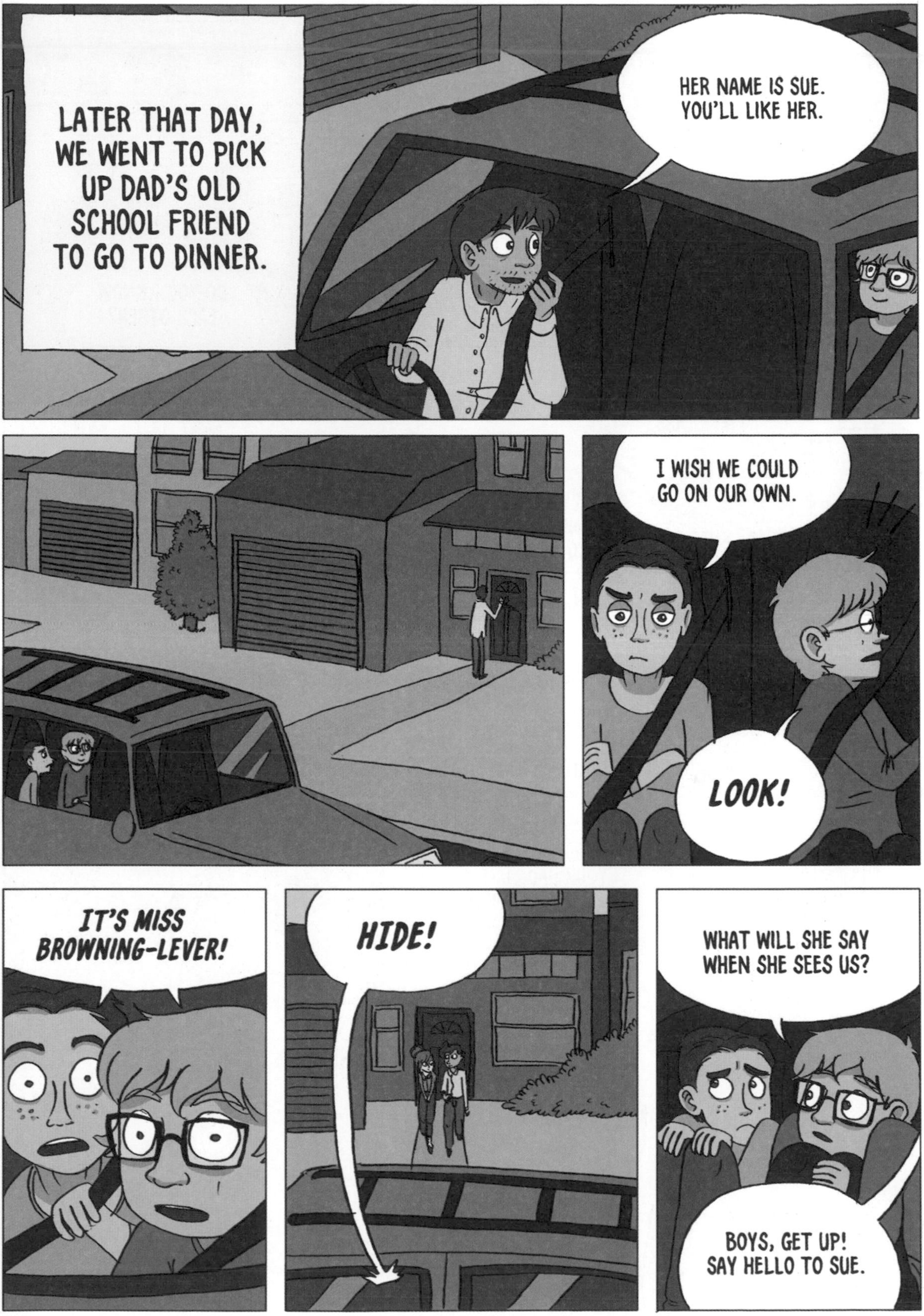
LATER THAT DAY, WE WENT TO PICK UP DAD'S OLD SCHOOL FRIEND TO GO TO DINNER.
HER NAME IS SUE. YOU'LL LIKE HER.
I WISH WE COULD GO ON OUR OWN.
LOOK!
IT'S MISS BROWNING-LEVER!
HIDE!
WHAT WILL SHE SAY WHEN SHE SEES US?
BOYS, GET UP! SAY HELLO TO SUE.

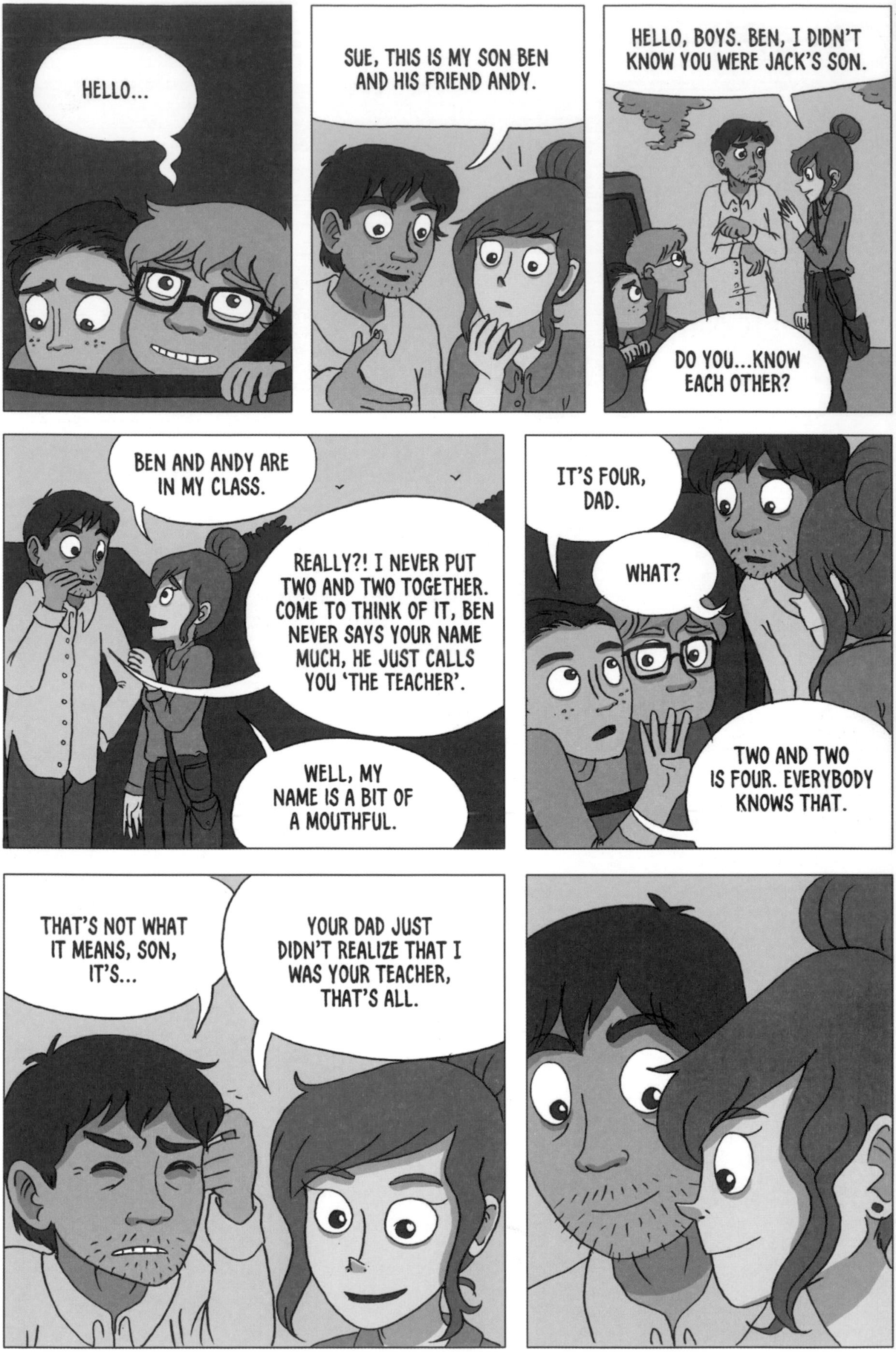
HELLO...
SUE, THIS IS MY SON BEN AND HIS FRIEND ANDY.
HELLO, BOYS. BEN, I DIDN'T KNOW YOU WERE JACK'S SON.
DO YOU...KNOW EACH OTHER?
BEN AND ANDY ARE IN MY CLASS.
REALLY?! I NEVER PUT TWO AND TWO TOGETHER. COME TO THINK OF IT, BEN NEVER SAYS YOUR NAME MUCH, HE JUST CALLS YOU 'THE TEACHER'.
WELL, MY NAME IS A BIT OF A MOUTHFUL.
IT'S FOUR, DAD.
WHAT?
TWO AND TWO IS FOUR. EVERYBODY KNOWS THAT.
THAT'S NOT WHAT IT MEANS, SON, IT'S...
YOUR DAD JUST DIDN'T REALIZE THAT I WAS YOUR TEACHER, THAT'S ALL.

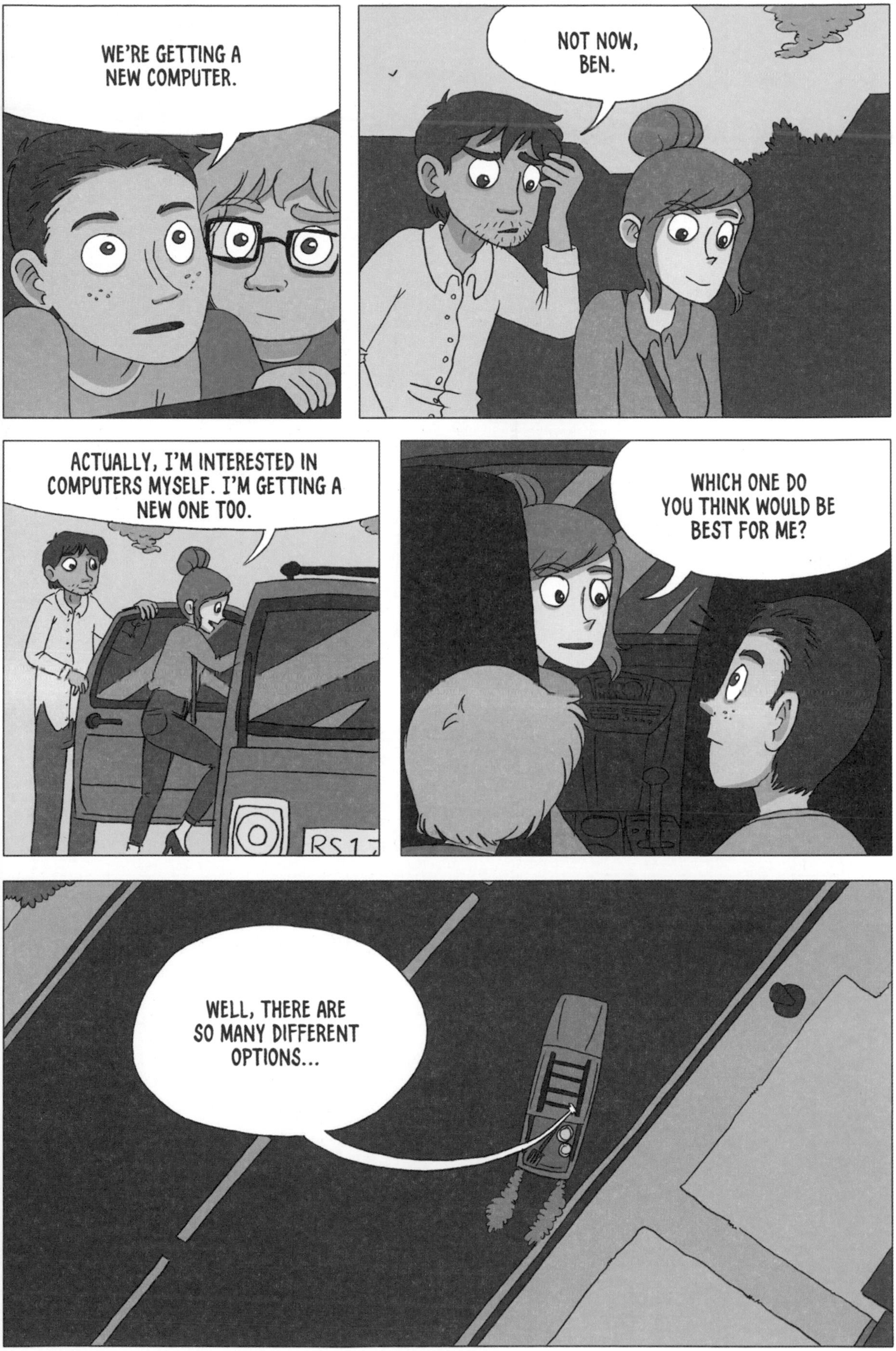
WE'RE GETTING A NEW COMPUTER.
NOT NOW, BEN.
ACTUALLY, I'M INTERESTED IN COMPUTERS MYSELF. I'M GETTING A NEW ONE TOO.
WHICH ONE DO YOU THINK WOULD BE BEST FOR ME?
WELL, THERE ARE SO MANY DIFFERENT OPTIONS...

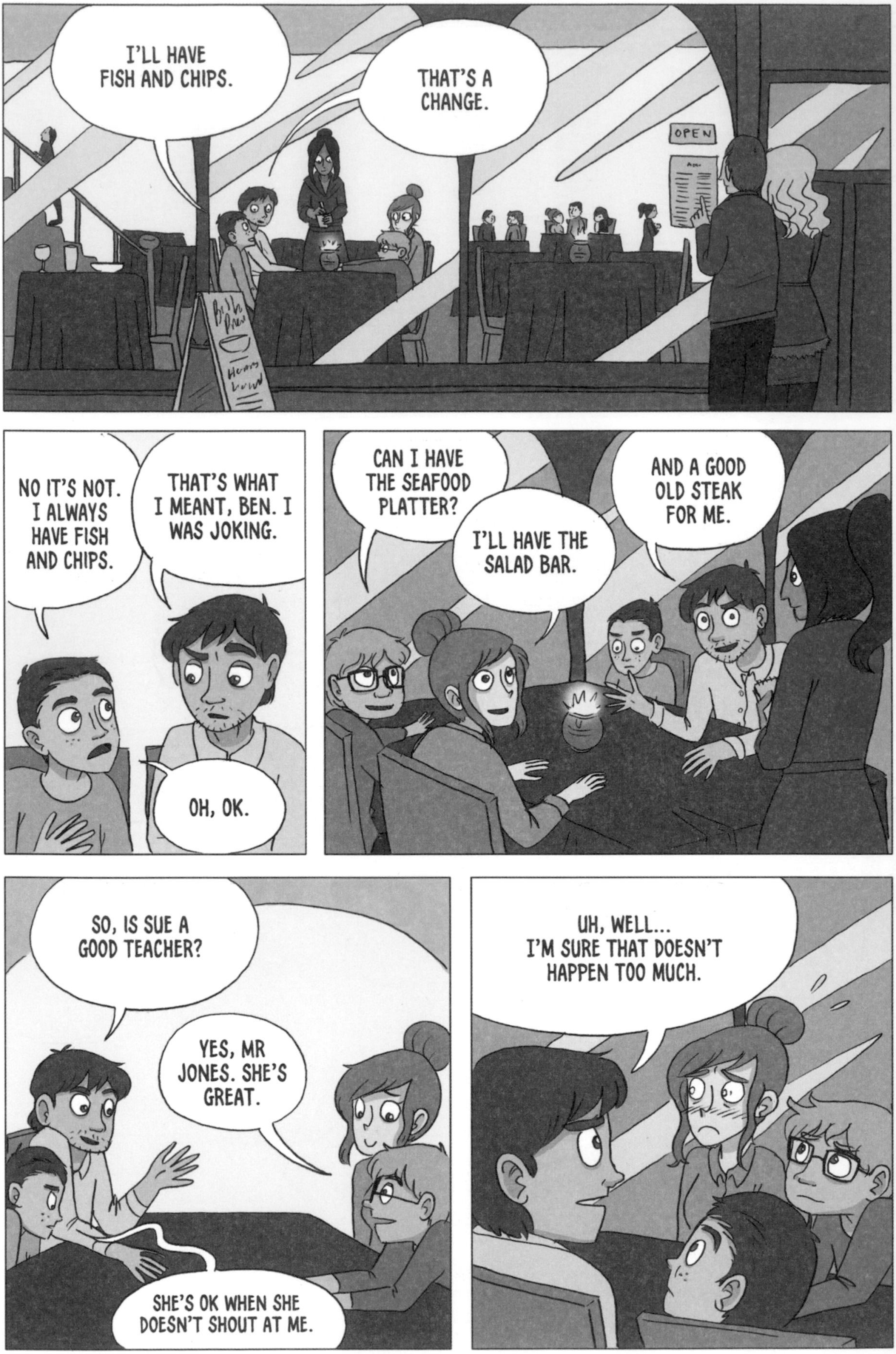
I'LL HAVE FISH AND CHIPS.
THAT'S A CHANGE.
OPEN
NO IT'S NOT. I ALWAYS HAVE FISH AND CHIPS.
THAT'S WHAT I MEANT, BEN. I WAS JOKING.
OH, OK.
CAN I HAVE THE SEAFOOD PLATTER?
I'LL HAVE THE SALAD BAR.
AND A GOOD OLD STEAK FOR ME.
SO, IS SUE A GOOD TEACHER?
YES, MR JONES. SHE'S GREAT.
SHE'S OK WHEN SHE DOESN'T SHOUT AT ME.
UH, WELL... I'M SURE THAT DOESN'T HAPPEN TOO MUCH.

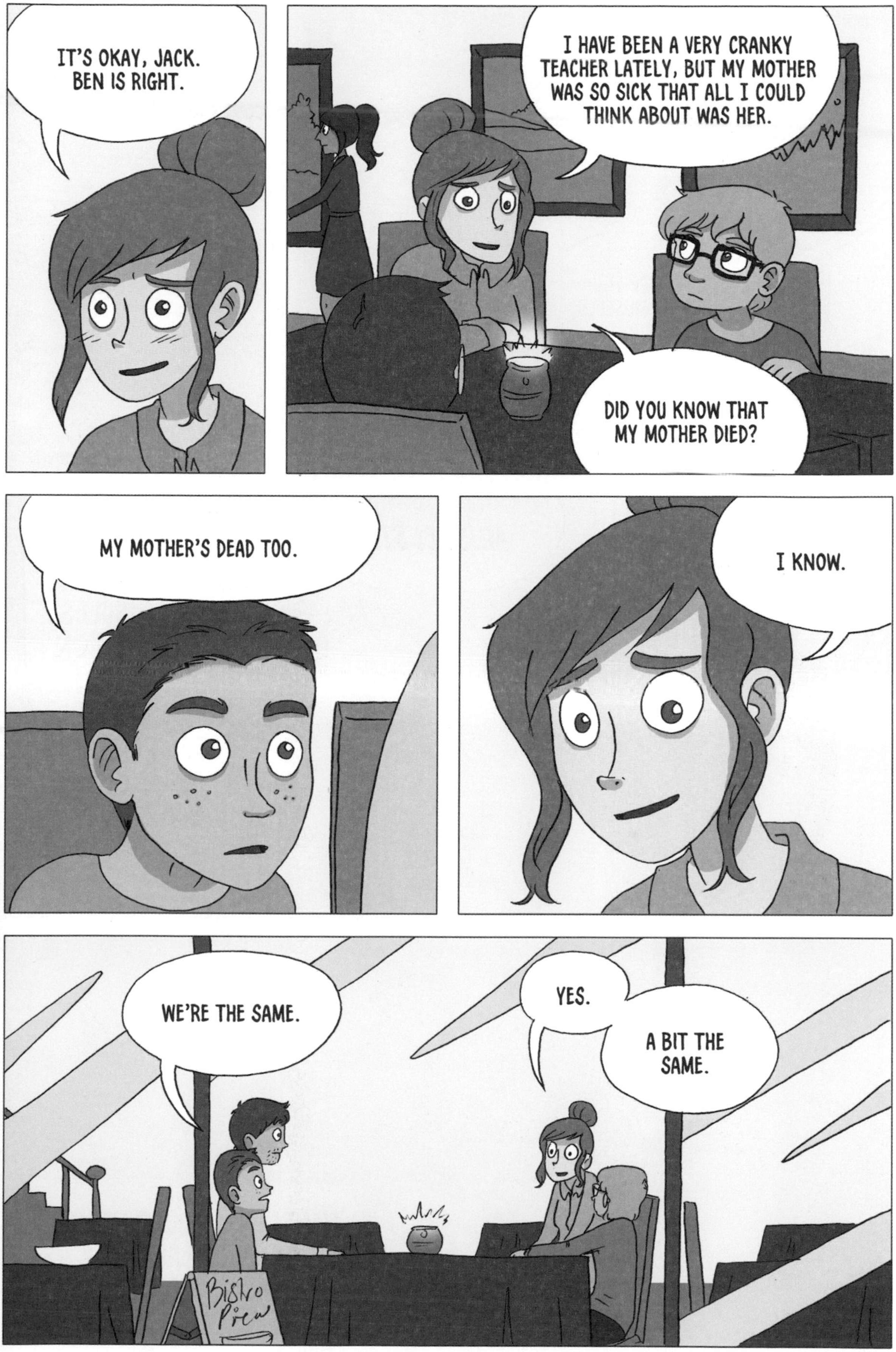
IT'S OKAY, JACK. BEN IS RIGHT.
I HAVE BEEN A VERY CRANKY TEACHER LATELY, BUT MY MOTHER WAS SO SICK THAT ALL I COULD THINK ABOUT WAS HER.
DID YOU KNOW THAT MY MOTHER DIED?
MY MOTHER'S DEAD TOO.
I KNOW.
WE'RE THE SAME.
YES.
A BIT THE SAME.
Bistro Prew

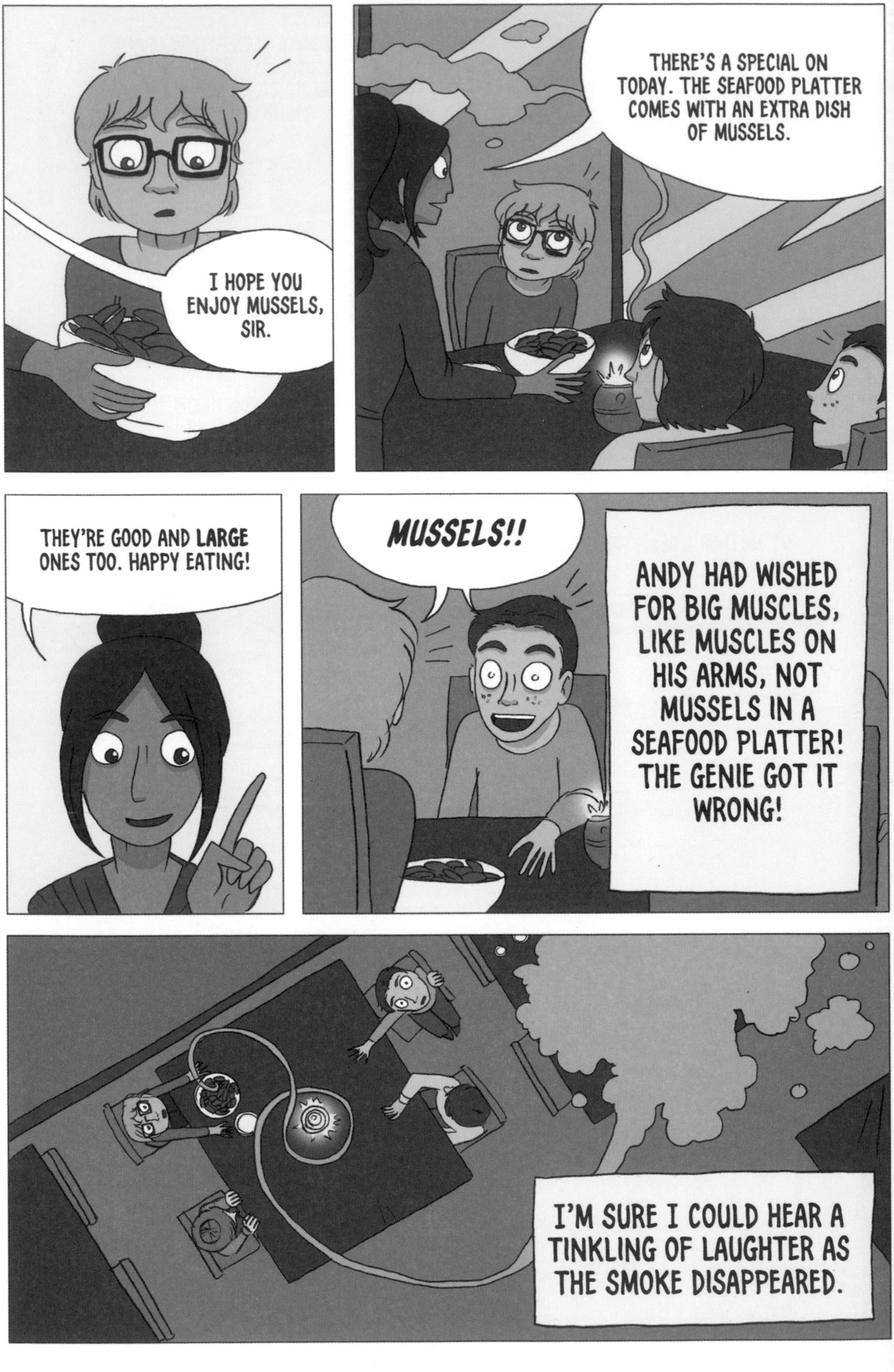
I HOPE YOU ENJOY MUSSELS, SIR.
THERE'S A SPECIAL ON TODAY. THE SEAFOOD PLATTER COMES WITH AN EXTRA DISH OF MUSSELS.
THEY'RE GOOD AND LARGE ONES TOO. HAPPY EATING!
MUSSELS!!
ANDY HAD WISHED FOR BIG MUSCLES, LIKE MUSCLES ON HIS ARMS, NOT MUSSELS IN A SEAFOOD PLATTER! THE GENIE GOT IT WRONG!
I'M SURE I COULD HEAR A TINKLING OF LAUGHTER AS THE SMOKE DISAPPEARED.

CHAPTER 11: THE NEW HOUSE

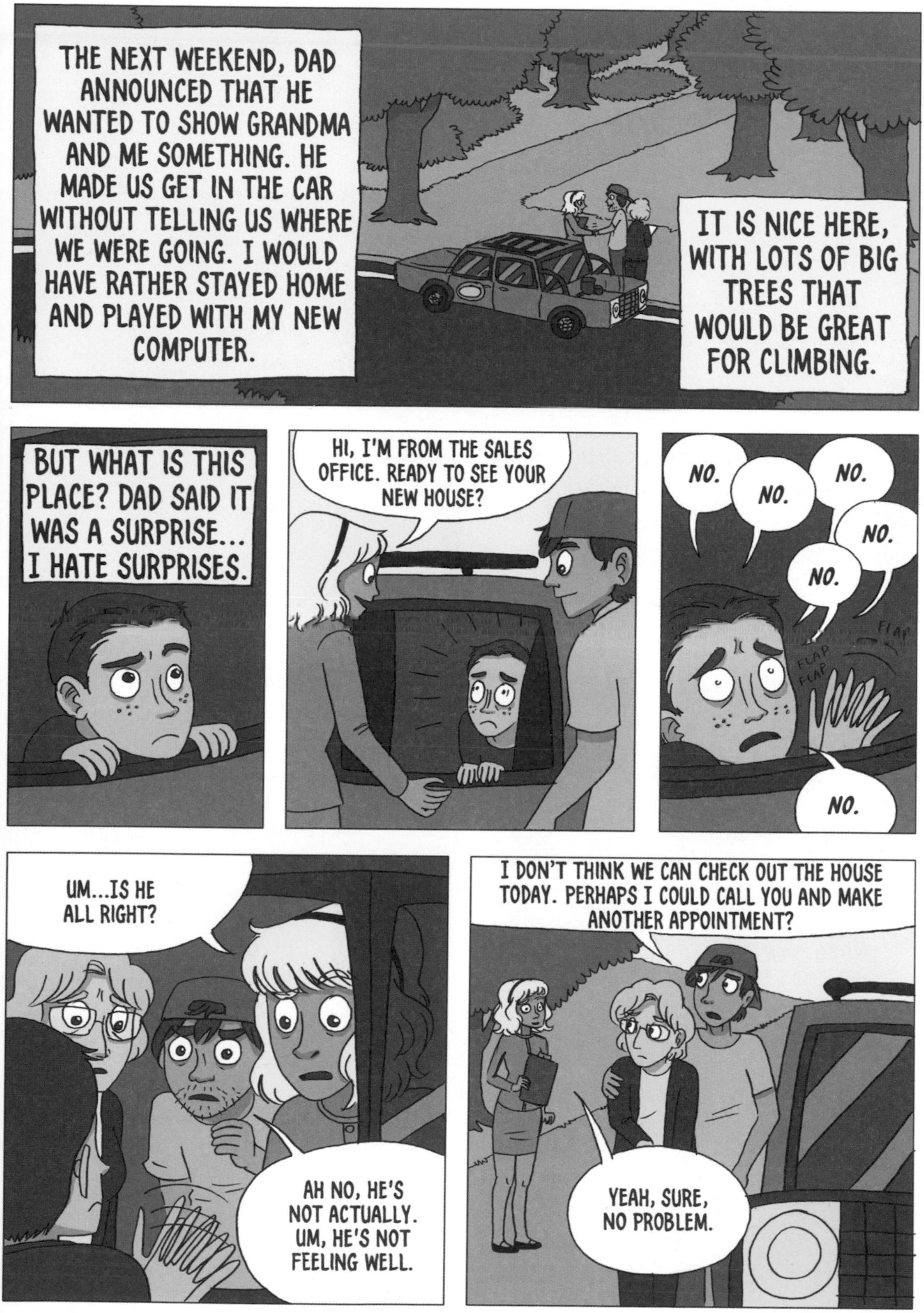

THE NEXT WEEKEND, DAD ANNOUNCED THAT HE WANTED TO SHOW GRANDMA AND ME SOMETHING. HE MADE US GET IN THE CAR WITHOUT TELLING US WHERE WE WERE GOING. I WOULD HAVE RATHER STAYED HOME AND PLAYED WITH MY NEW COMPUTER.
IT IS NICE HERE, WITH LOTS OF BIG TREES THAT WOULD BE GREAT FOR CLIMBING.
BUT WHAT IS THIS PLACE? DAD SAID IT WAS A SURPRISE... I HATE SURPRISES.
HI, I'M FROM THE SALES OFFICE. READY TO SEE YOUR NEW HOUSE?
NO.
NO.
NO.
NO.
NO.
FLAP
FLAP
FLAP
NO.
UM...IS HE ALL RIGHT?
AH NO, HE'S NOT ACTUALLY. UM, HE'S NOT FEELING WELL.
I DON'T THINK WE CAN CHECK OUT THE HOUSE TODAY. PERHAPS I COULD CALL YOU AND MAKE ANOTHER APPOINTMENT?
YEAH, SURE, NO PROBLEM.

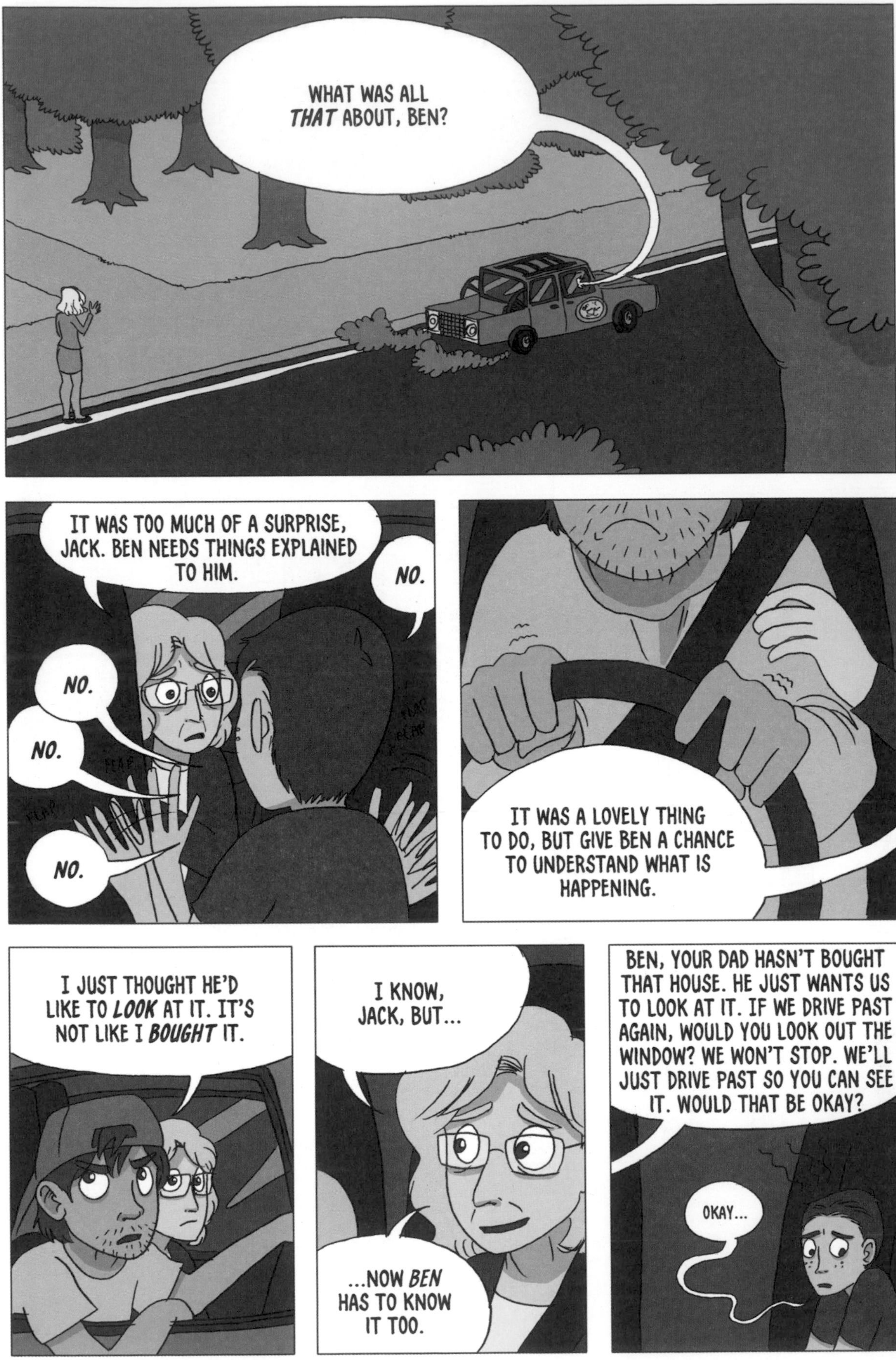
WHAT WAS ALL *THAT* ABOUT, BEN?
IT WAS TOO MUCH OF A SURPRISE, JACK. BEN NEEDS THINGS EXPLAINED TO HIM.
NO.
NO.
NO.
NO.
IT WAS A LOVELY THING TO DO, BUT GIVE BEN A CHANCE TO UNDERSTAND WHAT IS HAPPENING.
I JUST THOUGHT HE'D LIKE TO *LOOK* AT IT. IT'S NOT LIKE I *BOUGHT* IT.
I KNOW, JACK, BUT...
...NOW *BEN* HAS TO KNOW IT TOO.
BEN, YOUR DAD HASN'T BOUGHT THAT HOUSE. HE JUST WANTS US TO LOOK AT IT. IF WE DRIVE PAST AGAIN, WOULD YOU LOOK OUT THE WINDOW? WE WON'T STOP. WE'LL JUST DRIVE PAST SO YOU CAN SEE IT. WOULD THAT BE OKAY?
OKAY...

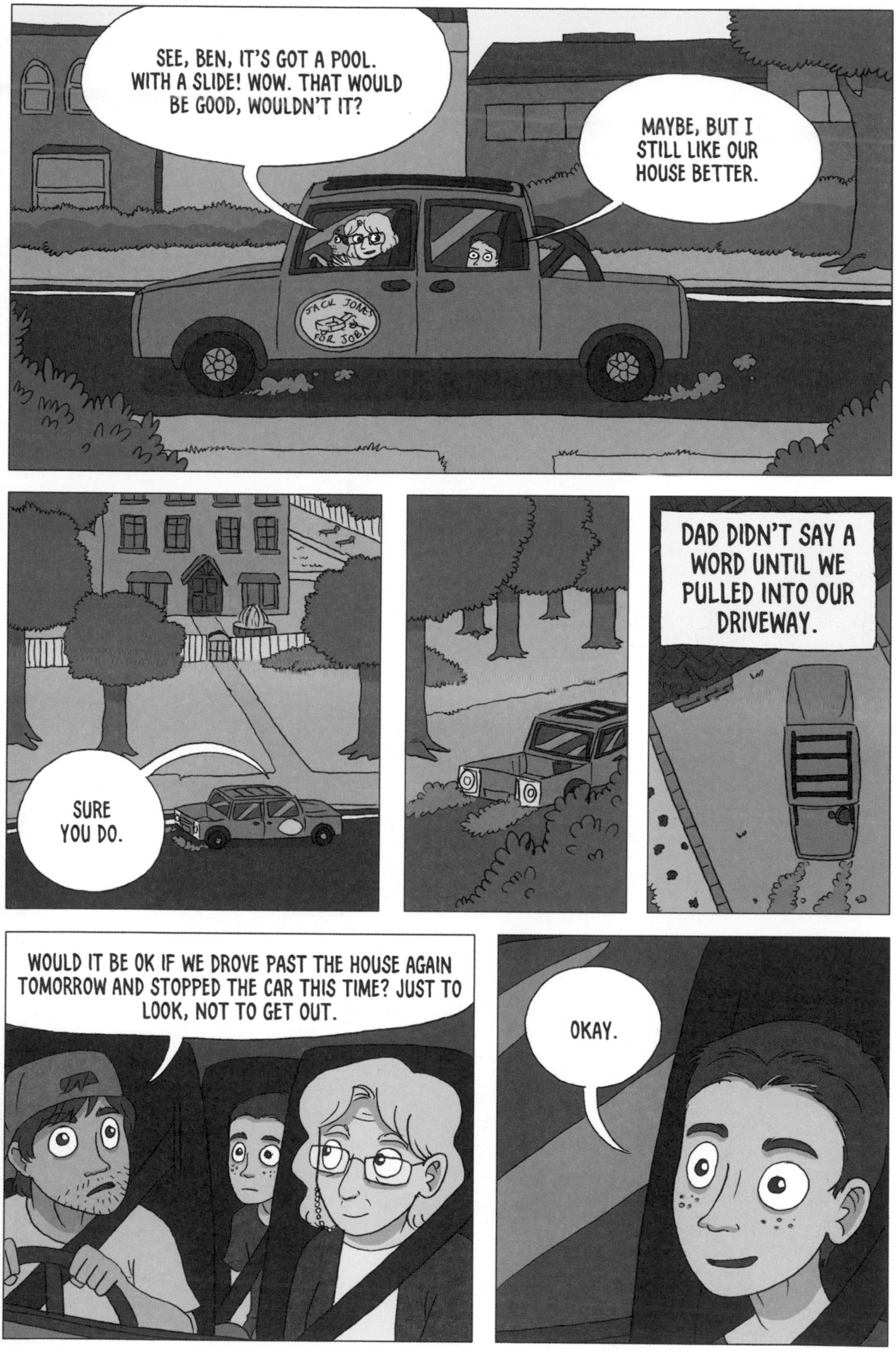
SEE, BEN, IT'S GOT A POOL. WITH A SLIDE! WOW. THAT WOULD BE GOOD, WOULDN'T IT?
MAYBE, BUT I STILL LIKE OUR HOUSE BETTER.
SURE YOU DO.
DAD DIDN'T SAY A WORD UNTIL WE PULLED INTO OUR DRIVEWAY.
WOULD IT BE OK IF WE DROVE PAST THE HOUSE AGAIN TOMORROW AND STOPPED THE CAR THIS TIME? JUST TO LOOK, NOT TO GET OUT.
OKAY.

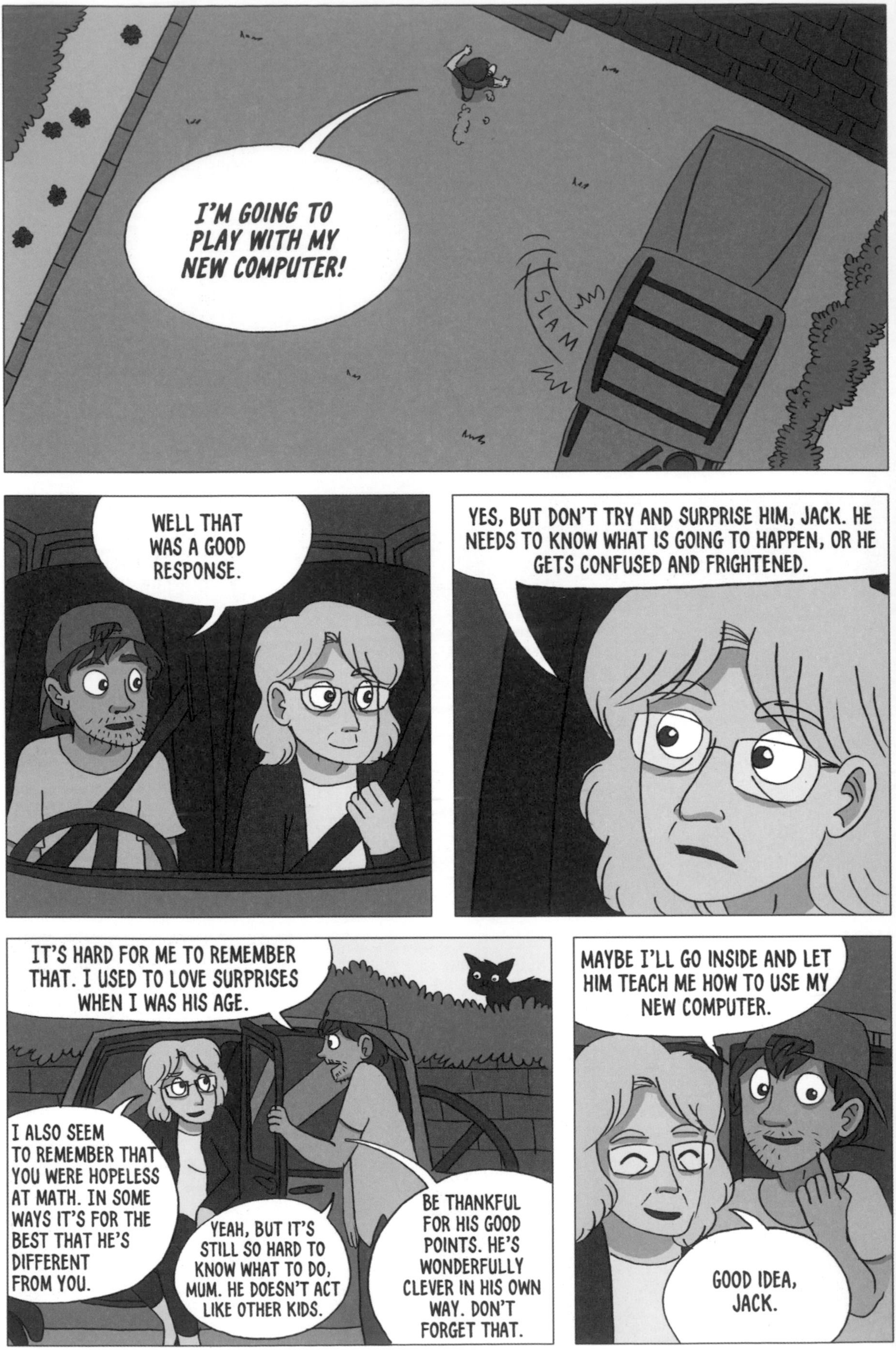
I'M GOING TO PLAY WITH MY NEW COMPUTER!
SLAM
WELL THAT WAS A GOOD RESPONSE.
YES, BUT DON'T TRY AND SURPRISE HIM, JACK. HE NEEDS TO KNOW WHAT IS GOING TO HAPPEN, OR HE GETS CONFUSED AND FRIGHTENED.
IT'S HARD FOR ME TO REMEMBER THAT. I USED TO LOVE SURPRISES WHEN I WAS HIS AGE.
I ALSO SEEM TO REMEMBER THAT YOU WERE HOPELESS AT MATH. IN SOME WAYS IT'S FOR THE BEST THAT HE'S DIFFERENT FROM YOU.
YEAH, BUT IT'S STILL SO HARD TO KNOW WHAT TO DO, MUM. HE DOESN'T ACT LIKE OTHER KIDS.
BE THANKFUL FOR HIS GOOD POINTS. HE'S WONDERFULLY CLEVER IN HIS OWN WAY. DON'T FORGET THAT.
MAYBE I'LL GO INSIDE AND LET HIM TEACH ME HOW TO USE MY NEW COMPUTER.
GOOD IDEA, JACK.

CHAPTER 12: THE HOUSE WARMING PARTY

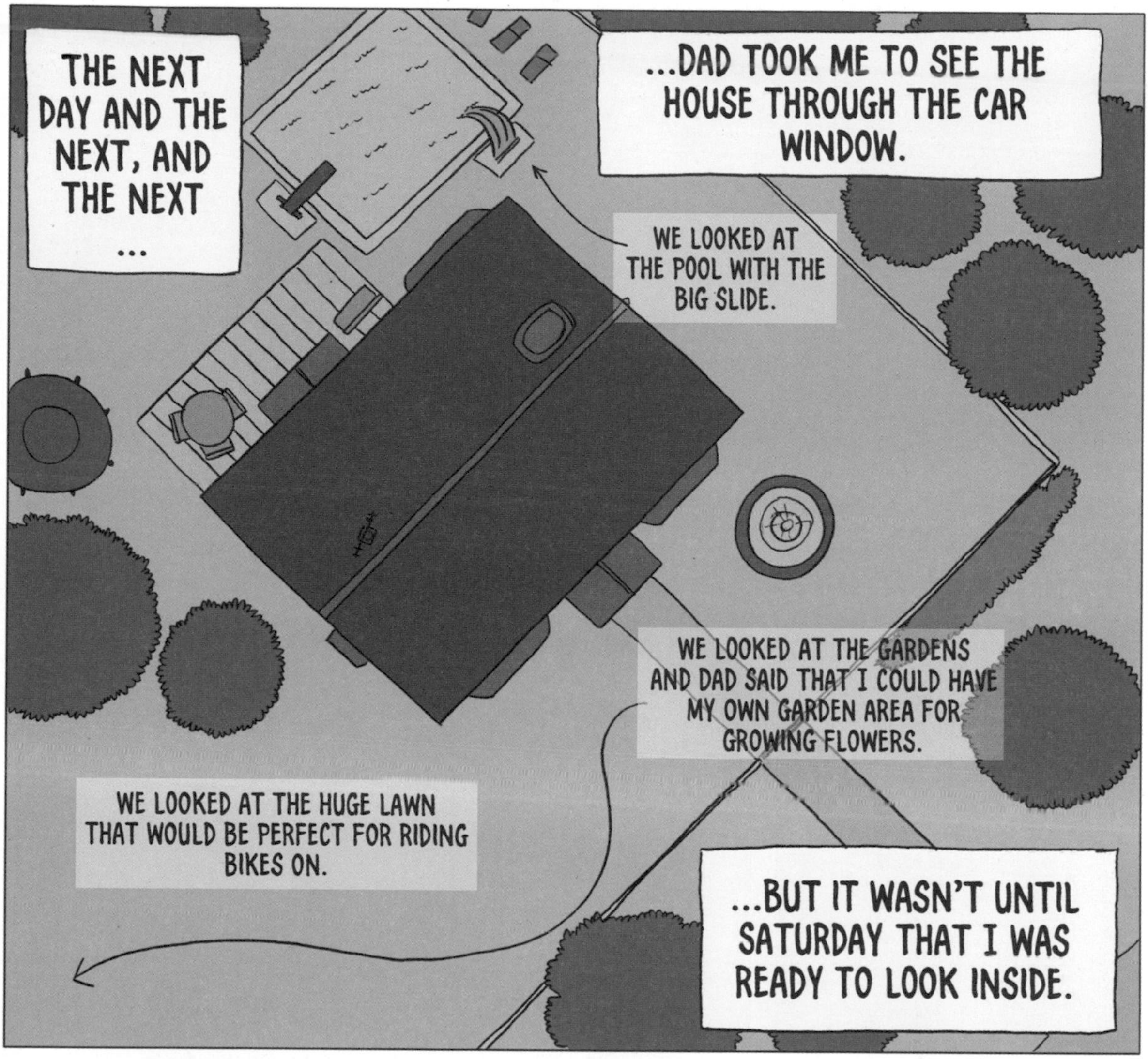
THE NEXT DAY AND THE NEXT, AND THE NEXT ...
...DAD TOOK ME TO SEE THE HOUSE THROUGH THE CAR WINDOW.
WE LOOKED AT THE POOL WITH THE BIG SLIDE.
WE LOOKED AT THE GARDENS AND DAD SAID THAT I COULD HAVE MY OWN GARDEN AREA FOR GROWING FLOWERS.
WE LOOKED AT THE HUGE LAWN THAT WOULD BE PERFECT FOR RIDING BIKES ON.
...BUT IT WASN'T UNTIL SATURDAY THAT I WAS READY TO LOOK INSIDE.

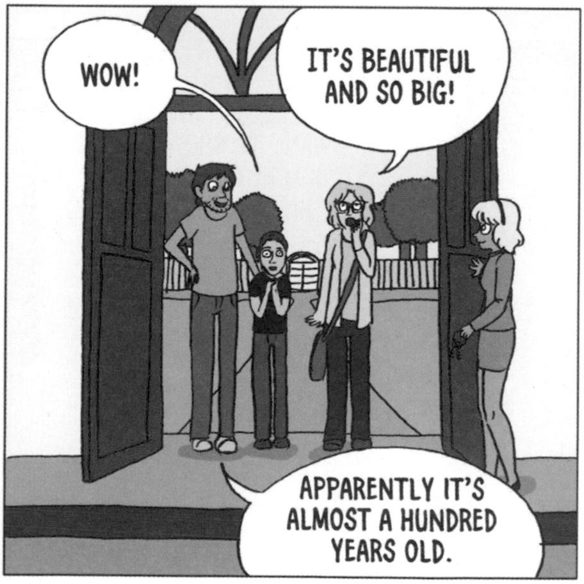
WOW!
IT'S BEAUTIFUL AND SO BIG!
APPARENTLY IT'S ALMOST A HUNDRED YEARS OLD.

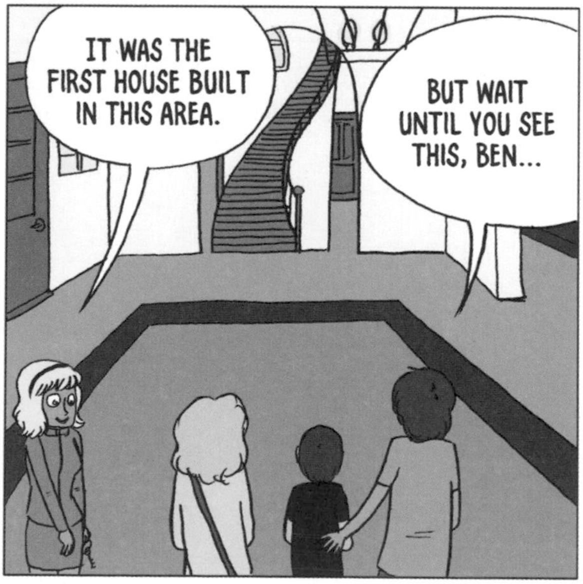
IT WAS THE FIRST HOUSE BUILT IN THIS AREA.
BUT WAIT UNTIL YOU SEE THIS, BEN...

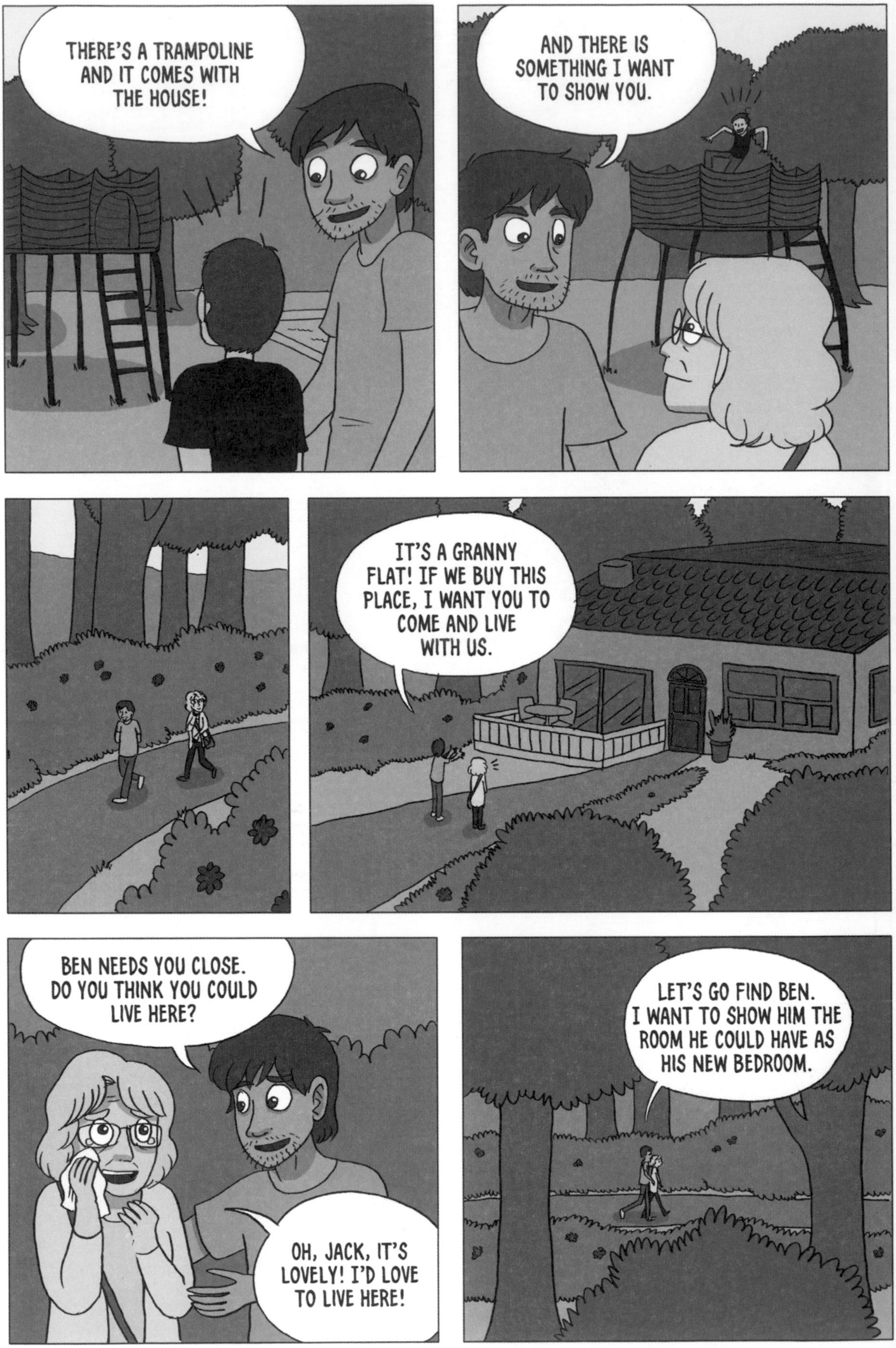

THERE'S A TRAMPOLINE AND IT COMES WITH THE HOUSE!
AND THERE IS SOMETHING I WANT TO SHOW YOU.
IT'S A GRANNY FLAT! IF WE BUY THIS PLACE, I WANT YOU TO COME AND LIVE WITH US.
BEN NEEDS YOU CLOSE. DO YOU THINK YOU COULD LIVE HERE?
OH, JACK, IT'S LOVELY! I'D LOVE TO LIVE HERE!
LET'S GO FIND BEN. I WANT TO SHOW HIM THE ROOM HE COULD HAVE AS HIS NEW BEDROOM.

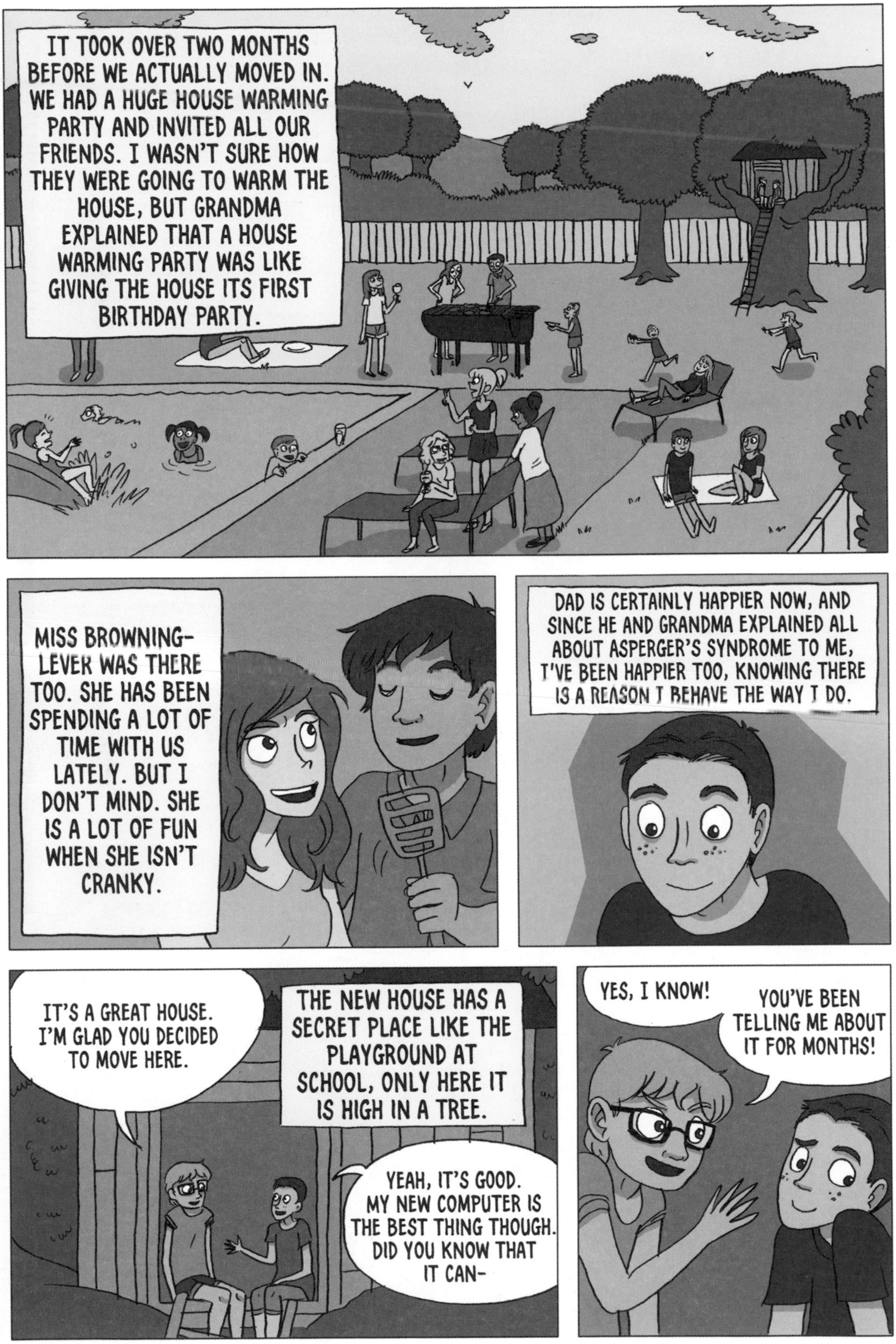
IT TOOK OVER TWO MONTHS BEFORE WE ACTUALLY MOVED IN. WE HAD A HUGE HOUSE WARMING PARTY AND INVITED ALL OUR FRIENDS. I WASN'T SURE HOW THEY WERE GOING TO WARM THE HOUSE, BUT GRANDMA EXPLAINED THAT A HOUSE WARMING PARTY WAS LIKE GIVING THE HOUSE ITS FIRST BIRTHDAY PARTY.
MISS BROWNING-LEVER WAS THERE TOO. SHE HAS BEEN SPENDING A LOT OF TIME WITH US LATELY. BUT I DON'T MIND. SHE IS A LOT OF FUN WHEN SHE ISN'T CRANKY.
DAD IS CERTAINLY HAPPIER NOW, AND SINCE HE AND GRANDMA EXPLAINED ALL ABOUT ASPERGER'S SYNDROME TO ME, I'VE BEEN HAPPIER TOO, KNOWING THERE IS A REASON I BEHAVE THE WAY I DO.
IT'S A GREAT HOUSE. I'M GLAD YOU DECIDED TO MOVE HERE.
THE NEW HOUSE HAS A SECRET PLACE LIKE THE PLAYGROUND AT SCHOOL, ONLY HERE IT IS HIGH IN A TREE.
YEAH, IT'S GOOD. MY NEW COMPUTER IS THE BEST THING THOUGH. DID YOU KNOW THAT IT CAN-
YES, I KNOW!
YOU'VE BEEN TELLING ME ABOUT IT FOR MONTHS!

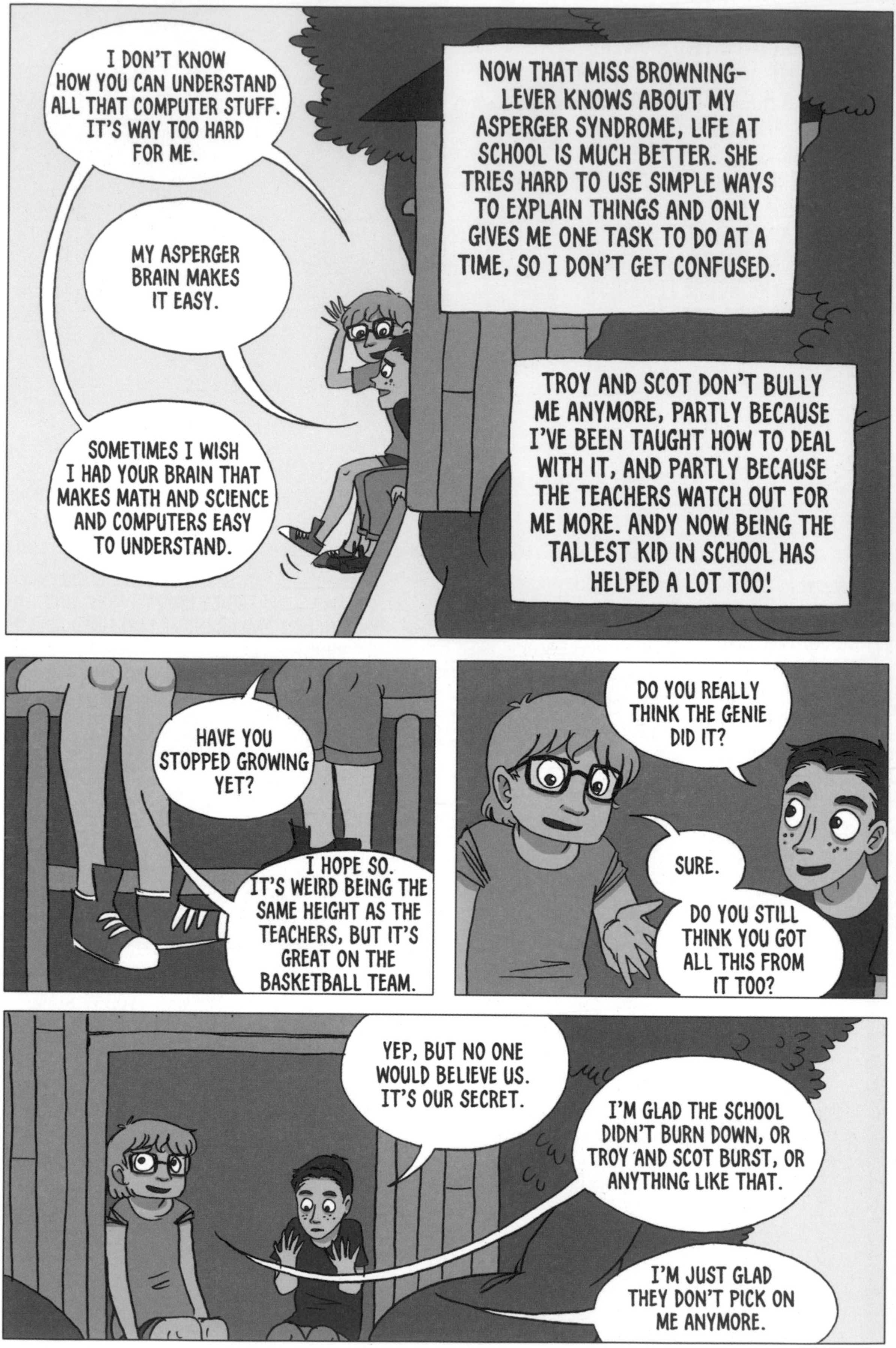
I DON'T KNOW HOW YOU CAN UNDERSTAND ALL THAT COMPUTER STUFF. IT'S WAY TOO HARD FOR ME.
NOW THAT MISS BROWNING-LEVER KNOWS ABOUT MY ASPERGER SYNDROME, LIFE AT SCHOOL IS MUCH BETTER. SHE TRIES HARD TO USE SIMPLE WAYS TO EXPLAIN THINGS AND ONLY GIVES ME ONE TASK TO DO AT A TIME, SO I DON'T GET CONFUSED.
MY ASPERGER BRAIN MAKES IT EASY.
SOMETIMES I WISH I HAD YOUR BRAIN THAT MAKES MATH AND SCIENCE AND COMPUTERS EASY TO UNDERSTAND.
TROY AND SCOT DON'T BULLY ME ANYMORE, PARTLY BECAUSE I'VE BEEN TAUGHT HOW TO DEAL WITH IT, AND PARTLY BECAUSE THE TEACHERS WATCH OUT FOR ME MORE. ANDY NOW BEING THE TALLEST KID IN SCHOOL HAS HELPED A LOT TOO!
HAVE YOU STOPPED GROWING YET?
I HOPE SO. IT'S WEIRD BEING THE SAME HEIGHT AS THE TEACHERS, BUT IT'S GREAT ON THE BASKETBALL TEAM.
DO YOU REALLY THINK THE GENIE DID IT?
SURE.
DO YOU STILL THINK YOU GOT ALL THIS FROM IT TOO?
YEP, BUT NO ONE WOULD BELIEVE US. IT'S OUR SECRET.
I'M GLAD THE SCHOOL DIDN'T BURN DOWN, OR TROY AND SCOT BURST, OR ANYTHING LIKE THAT.
I'M JUST GLAD THEY DON'T PICK ON ME ANYMORE.

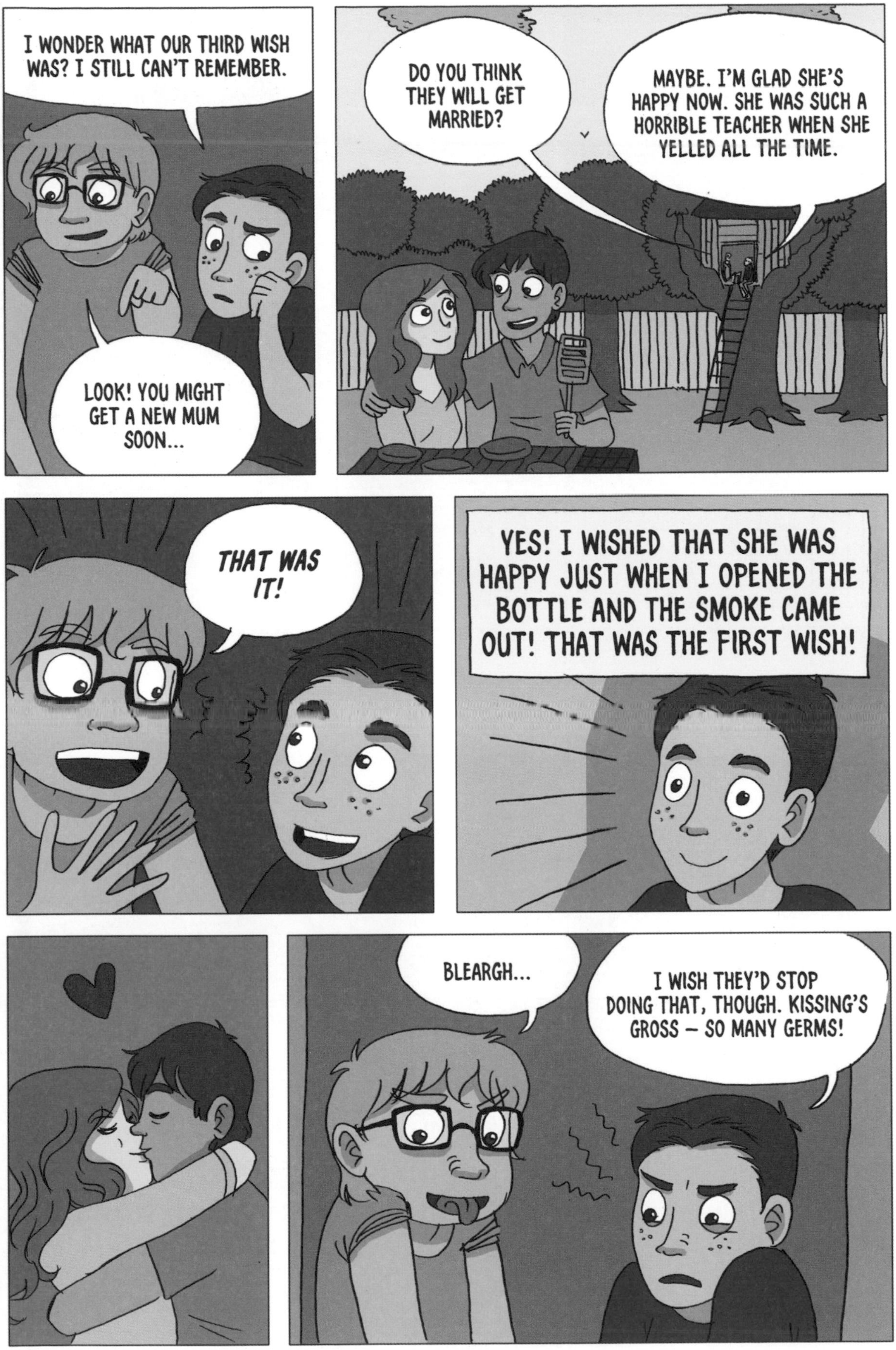
I WONDER WHAT OUR THIRD WISH WAS? I STILL CAN'T REMEMBER.
LOOK! YOU MIGHT GET A NEW MUM SOON...
DO YOU THINK THEY WILL GET MARRIED?
MAYBE. I'M GLAD SHE'S HAPPY NOW. SHE WAS SUCH A HORRIBLE TEACHER WHEN SHE YELLED ALL THE TIME.
THAT WAS IT!
YES! I WISHED THAT SHE WAS HAPPY JUST WHEN I OPENED THE BOTTLE AND THE SMOKE CAME OUT! THAT WAS THE FIRST WISH!
BLEARGH...
I WISH THEY'D STOP DOING THAT, THOUGH. KISSING'S GROSS – SO MANY GERMS!

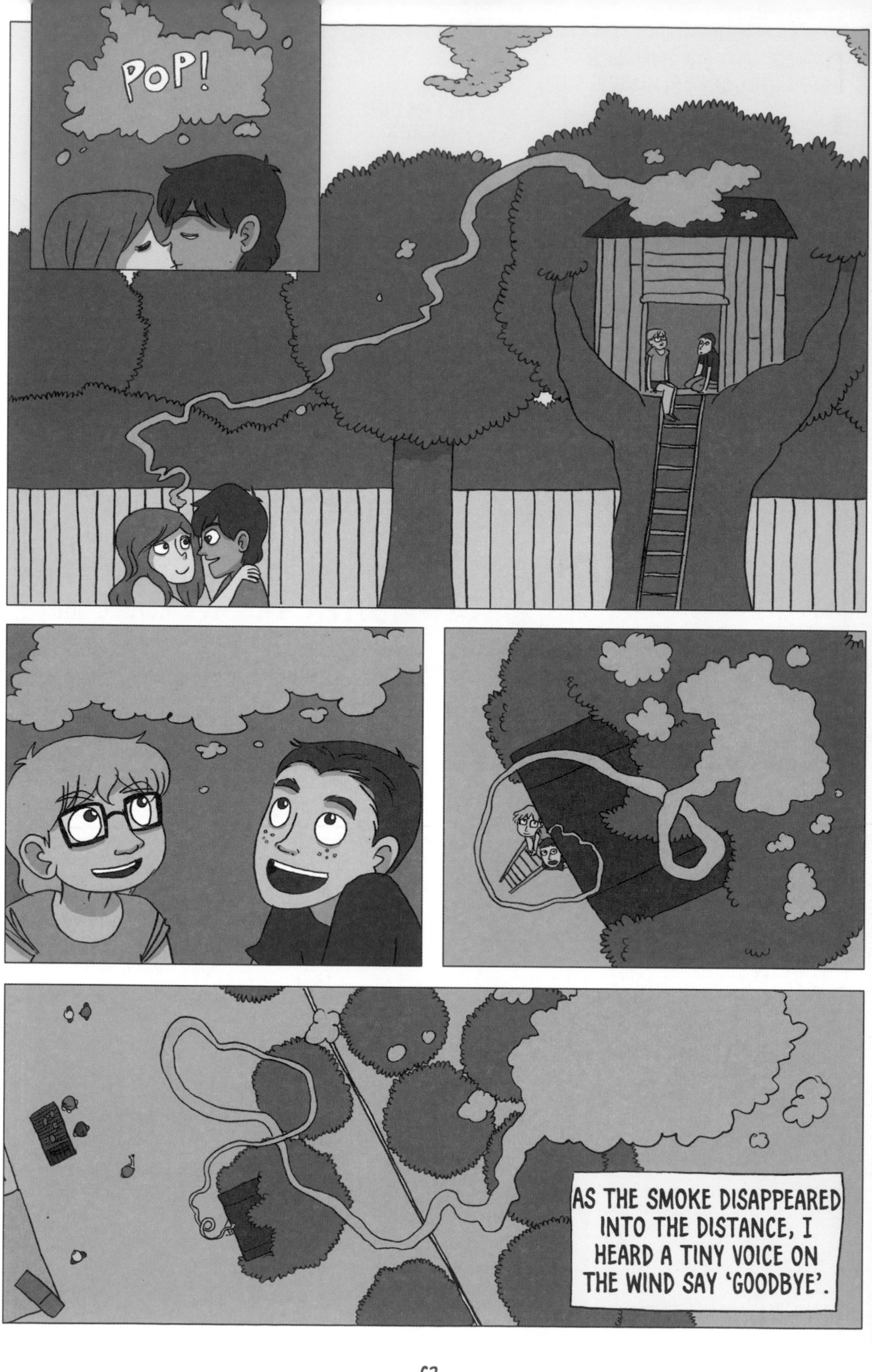
POP!
AS THE SMOKE DISAPPEARED INTO THE DISTANCE, I HEARD A TINY VOICE ON THE WIND SAY 'GOODBYE'.

EPILOGUE: ONE YEAR LATER...

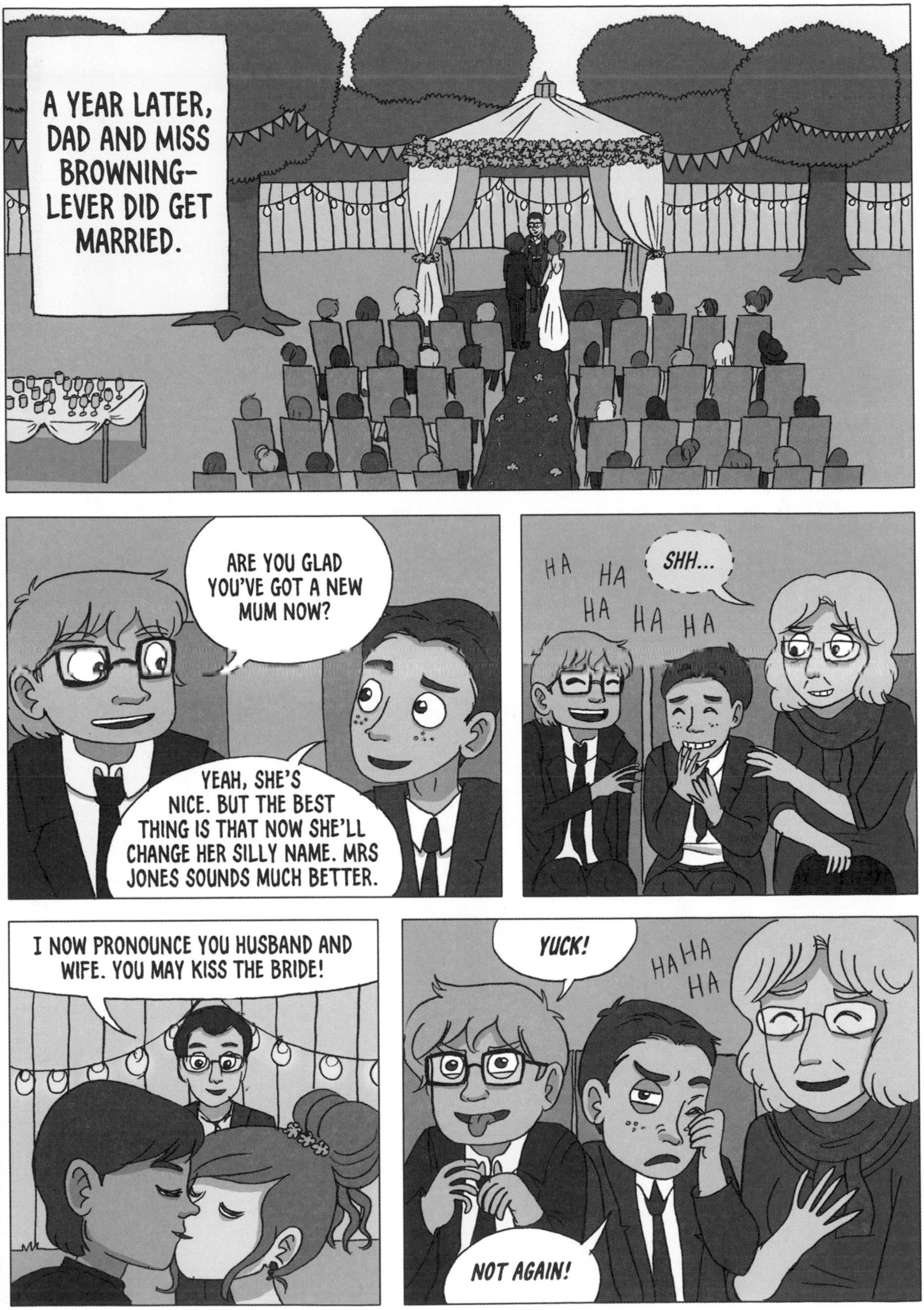
A YEAR LATER, DAD AND MISS BROWNING-LEVER DID GET MARRIED.
ARE YOU GLAD YOU'VE GOT A NEW MUM NOW?
YEAH, SHE'S NICE. BUT THE BEST THING IS THAT NOW SHE'LL CHANGE HER SILLY NAME. MRS JONES SOUNDS MUCH BETTER.
HA HA HA HA HA HA
SHH...
I NOW PRONOUNCE YOU HUSBAND AND WIFE. YOU MAY KISS THE BRIDE!
YUCK!
HA HA HA
NOT AGAIN!

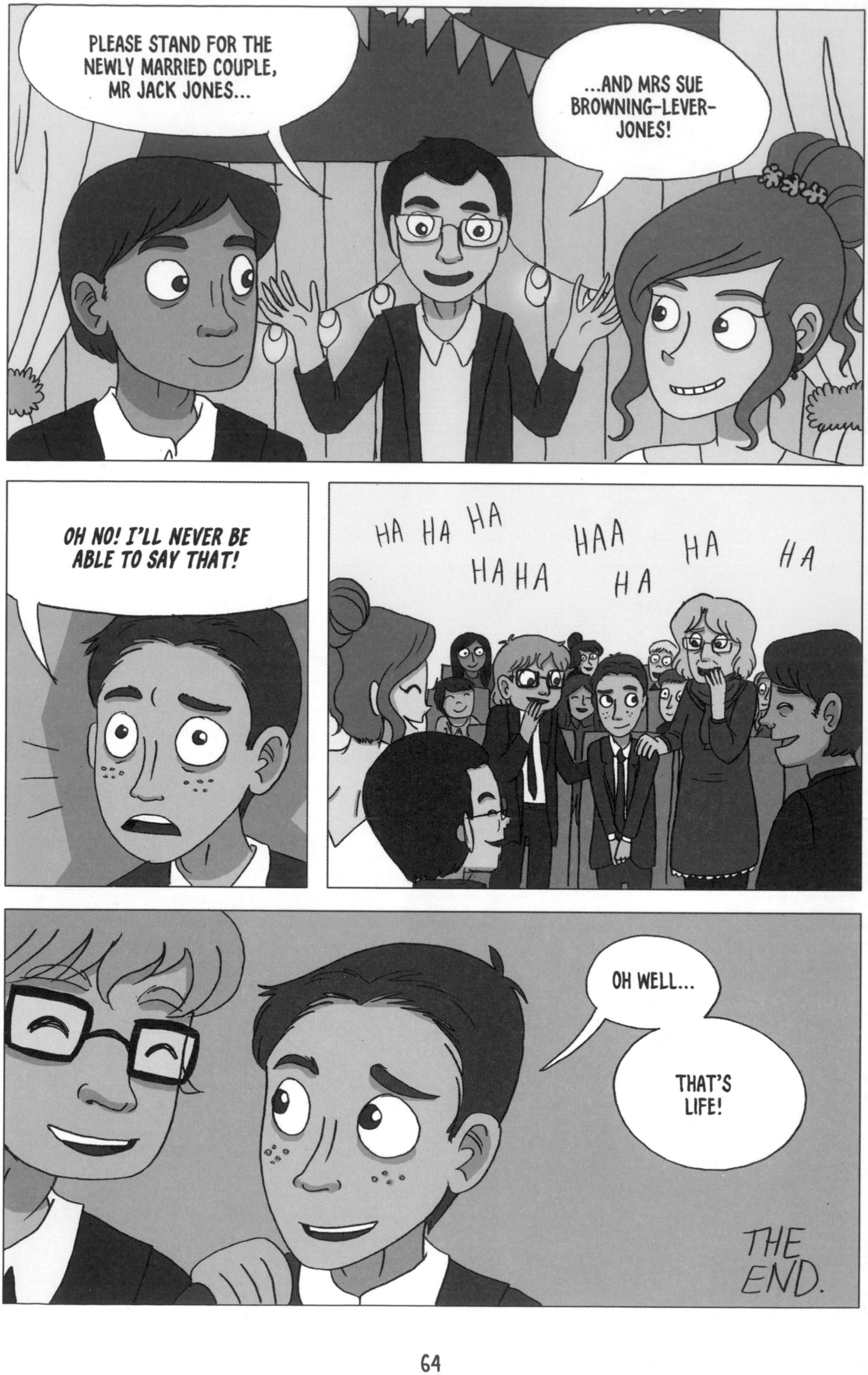
PLEASE STAND FOR THE NEWLY MARRIED COUPLE, MR JACK JONES...
...AND MRS SUE BROWNING-LEVER-JONES!
OH NO! I'LL NEVER BE ABLE TO SAY THAT!
HA HA HA
HAA
HA
HA
HA HA
HA
OH WELL...
THAT'S LIFE!
THE END.